WHEN I WAS A FATHER
Alvaro Cardona-Hine

Previous books by the author

Romance de Agapito Cascante, Ediciones Repertorio Americano, San Jose, Costa Rica

The Gathering Wave, Alan Swallow, Denver

The Flesh of Utopia, Alan Swallow, Denver

Menashtash, Little Square Review Press, Santa Barbara, California

Agapito, Charles Scribners' Sons

Spain, Let This Cup Pass From Me, (Translation of Cesar Vallejo) Red Hill Press, California

Words on Paper, Red Hill Press, California

Two Elegies, Red Hill Press, California

The Half-Eaten Angel, Nodin Press, Minnesota

Alvaro Cardona-Hine

WHEN I WAS A FATHER

Minnesota Voices Project #7

New Rivers Press

List of Illustrations:

Front cover: Elena
Pages 5 and 6: Karen
Pages 10 and 12: Elena
Pages 32 and 33: Miguel
Pages 49 and 50: Alvaro Modesto
Pages 63 and 65: Aglaia
Back cover: Aglaia

Copyright © 1982 by Alvaro Cardona-Hine
Library of Congress Catalog Card Number: 82-80604
ISBN: 0-89823-036-5
All rights reserved
Book design: C. W. Truesdale
Typesetting: Peregrine Cold Type

This publication was made possible in part by a grant provided by the Metropolitan Council from funds appropriated by the Minnesota State Legislature and by a grant from the Arts Development Fund. Special thanks to Bill Jamieson for color separations.

The writing of this book, long in the making, was finally made possible thanks to a fellowship from the Bush Foundation.

New Rivers Press books are distributed by:

Small Press Distribution, Inc.   &   Bookslinger
1784 Shattuck Avenue   330 East 9th Street
Berkeley, CA 94709   St. Paul, MN 55101

When I Was A Father has been manufactured in the United States of America for New Rivers Press, Inc. (C. W. Truesdale, editor/publisher), 1602 Selby Avenue, St. Paul, MN 55104 in a first edition of 1000 copies, of which 50 have been bound in boards and signed and numbered by the author and 950 in wrappers.

to Karen
my one and only step-daughter
who always
from the very first
called my children her brothers

To: Daddy

On your day time is free busy, busy, busy like a little squirrel climbing on your ladder here, no I think over there!

Happy Father's Day

Love,
Karen

Happy Brithday alvaro! Love karen

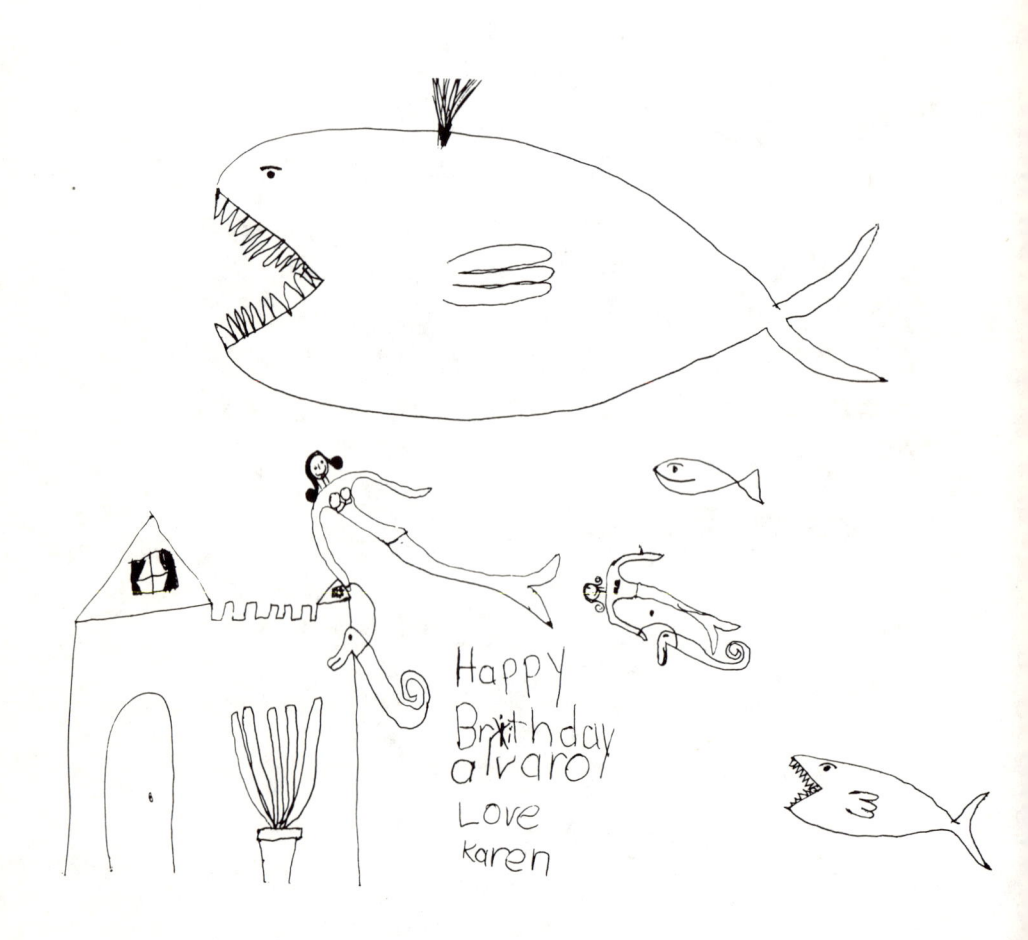

introduction

THERE IS A HIDDEN WORLD FROM WHICH MY CHILDREN were drawn, as there is this territory of wonder and sorrow we have traversed together. By listening carefully, with my whole being, to the distance between me and my children, I have discovered a few things about them and about our relationship which might be good to tell. I have also wanted to let them know where I have come from (garbed, like them, in this why-business for which there is no because) and knowing that what I said —even if steeped in clarities— would comfort them.

Each of us is a pure spirit, dressed slowly by itself in flesh, veiled and profound as laughter and tears. How, then, does one go about capturing something of its essence?

I have come to believe, oh, most happily, that the irresistible ebb and flow of life has little to do with chronology. We should know by now that time is the loom on which we are free to weave designs of ecstasy and surprise. It is not essential to consciousness but a manifestation of it; and we should never be its slaves, for only slaves believe in death. Therefore, this work is set down in the liberated form of the *haibun*, as the Japanese would call it: prose interspersed with *haiku* the serious and *senryu* the smiling —even some *tanka*, all in memory of kin and self and place, schoolmate, friend and moustachioed barber (the one on Main Street), hushed and inorganic now. It is a shirt, a spirit shirt, whose buttons, as key points in the space of emotion, condense in poetry.

Still, nothing takes shape without that underlying loom. Here are its lineaments so that the reader might feel more comfortable with the capriciousness of the work:

I was born in Costa Rica in 1926, living the wonderful life of childhood alternately in farms (San Isidro and San Antonio) and town until our parents brought me and my sister to Los Angeles in 1940.

In 1950 I married my first wife, whose family lived in the small town of Ellensburg, Washington. First, as newlyweds, we went to Costa Rica for a few months, hoping to enter Mexico as residents so that I could study music there. We had temporarily abandoned the United States because of the oppressive political climate of the time. When we did get to Mexico it was only as tourists and I studied illegally for a while at the National Conservatory. Our first son, Alvaro Modesto, was conceived there but he was born in Ellensburg, where my wife had gone to be with her dying mother. Since I couldn't work in Mexico I had no choice but to return to the United States in order to support the three of us. We lived in Ellensburg for five years while I worked for the local college. Aglaia was born exactly a year after Pigo (the nickname I gave my son for eating so heartily during his infancy). We returned to Los Angeles in 1957 and I went to work for an insurance company. For nine years I suffered that job at a ridiculous rate of pay, then tried, for two more years, to sell insurance. Nonetheless, more happiness arrived, first in the form of Elena, born in 1958, and then with Miguel, who came in 1962.

In 1967 my wife and I separated and my role as a father took on new meanings and direction. My children and I are even to this day discovering who we are; sometimes I tell them where I come from, other times they tell me where an origin occurs. We are confused, we are clear.

            ach
            St. Paul, Minnesota
            January 5, 1979

WHEN I WAS A FATHER

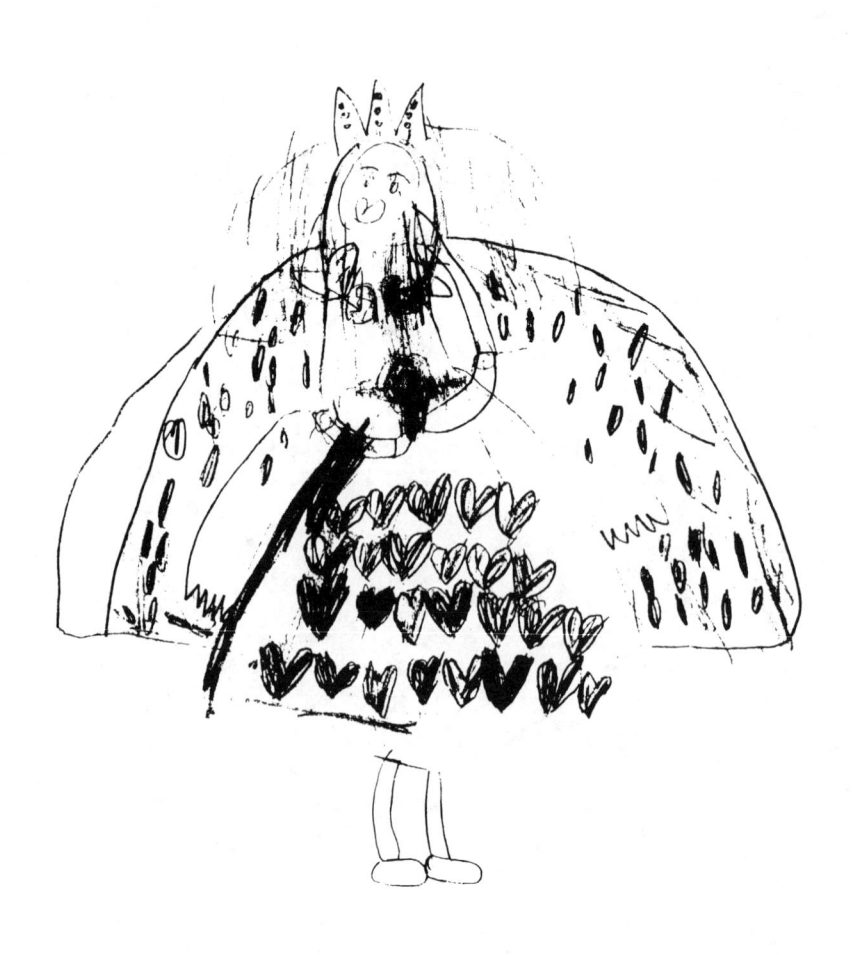

It is Sunday. Outside, a rain which threatens to pale and turn into snow. The light of the afternoon is a withered turnip. I have found time to please my girl.

>   *a flash of lightning*
> *I sit*
> >   *painting the eyebrows*
> *on Aglaia's doll*

    Yes, it is almost winter. Soon, there will be nothing to do but burn wood and listen to the flakes of snow delivering themselves in huge shipments of softness. In the yard of this small house we've bought with my mother's help, the lilac bushes have forgotten the green light after an April rain; the apple tree doesn't have the static of a single bee in its bonnet, let alone the hundreds it will have when it becomes a bride in May. It stands out there casting no shadow, dreaming itself a component in some Hiroshige print of mountainous location.
    "Are you going to put arms on my doll?" she asks.
    Children want so much. I should never have picked up this thalidomide effigy I found on the way home one day.
    "Imagine an armless doll standing in the snow, Aglaia. Potentially, it is directing traffic, but the embrace is elsewhere."
    She looks at me. Why do I talk to her as if she were a twenty-year-old?
    Look, children, I had no business putting together this book in the first place, no business arriving at the sum total of a smile at the end of endless columns of numbers; but there were so many stop lights in the life of your father, so many moments when the boss' back was turned, that I could not resist. And I had to show the world that it could not make a silent working cypher out of me. As the style evolved, this gnarled story-telling way peculiar to necessity, *haiku* would take shape beneath the insurance papers, memory would be among the packages I would have to deliver... it was never an orderly business, a timely affair...

> *besides*
> >   *these haiku*
> *they are*
> >   *how else to put it?*
> *my other children*

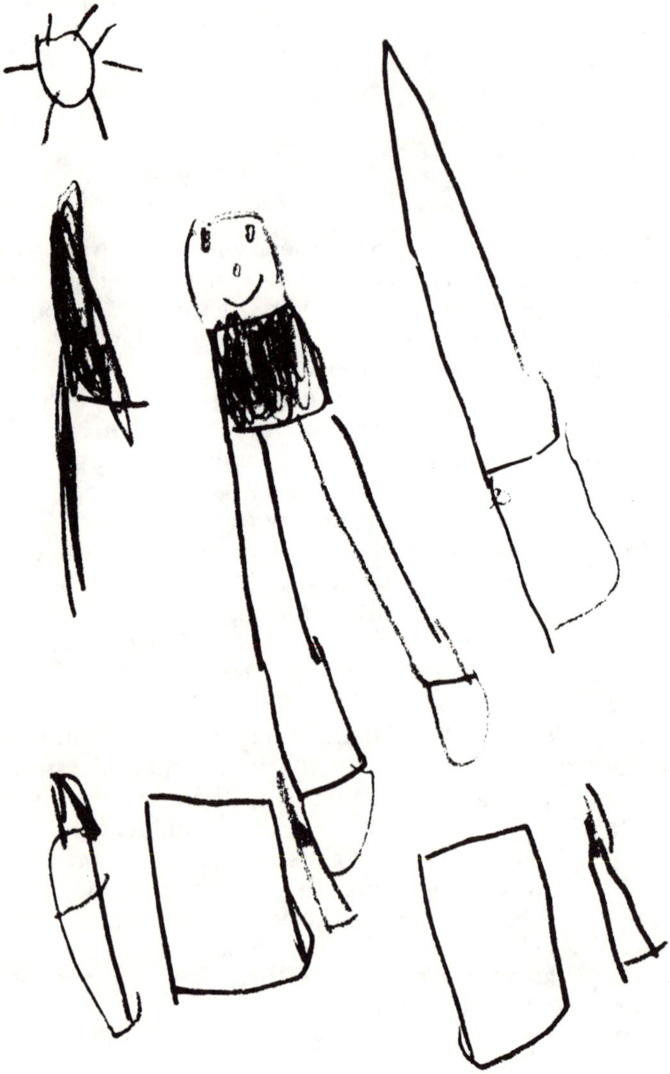

MY WIFE AND I WERE MARRIED AND WANTED A MEADOW; our first born should be a meadow, meadow of want, curved like a body of want. Of silence, loud as a wave.

At night we used to steal out and gather the necessary dew. In buckets of years and yesterdays, the springs of the hammock joining the bugs' summer festival, in armfuls.

We talked to doves, exchanging continents (they coo coeval to this morning, sad with joy); we talked to strangers, what's legal and tender, through the screen door of their private domain.

He was too late, for one thing, to enjoy two grandmothers. Only the paternal grandmother lived to see him. The other, in whose house he began to develop human attributes, had passed away just months before.

> *your mother's mother*
> *would have scrubbed you in the sink*
> *her bit of china*

I recall one Saturday or Sunday morning when I was trying to catch up on my sleep. Pigo must have been four or five weeks old; his mother had placed him on our bed in order to change his diapers, and, while she was getting a new set from the laundry basket in the next room, she left him uncovered for a few moments. The cold air of the room must have triggered his bladder, for the next thing I knew —vaguely, in my dream— was that a warm, brackish summer rain was falling on my face. Still half dozing, I put my hand up to guard off the insistent shower but to no avail. Opening my eyes I saw the jet of pee emanating from his gherkin-like penis, describing a wide arc in the air and falling on me with incredible accuracy; a veritable Italian fountain.

And Aglaia? When she was about two and we went to see the fourth of July fireworks just outside of town, she was caught up in the wonder of color, turned to me and, throwing her arms around my neck, exclaimed, "Daddy, I love you for joy!"

Yes, our second child should be a daughter, film of sky on the surface of a sleeping lake. She came with the rain, the sweet morose look, half a mile above the river's rim, where the water contends against a thousand boulders. Or sleeps the summers by, trickling past the compacted grain of the mountain.

In my land, too, there was a river, the river out back, knocking itself out against a thousand boulders. In the mornings the sun shines, the oxcarts rumble by (or used to, before the Diesel fumes took over). The peasant children walk down the road to school, white shirts and blue pants all —or white blouses and blue skirts— their bare feet somehow immaculately clean.

When we wanted another girl, her lungs would be shaped in the womb, her tiny fingernails stolen wildberries from a slope of the Diamond Sutra. She had to be one who could snow around you, Greek in grace, orange after an orange girl: Elena.

Elena, my second girl, my third child, my girl child Elena 2... where is she in that green enclosure of a patio that all I see are lemons and hummingbirds and a golden snow? Butterflies come and sit on her head like effete manufacturers of silk. Hummingbirds suspend the passage of the afternoon to drink from her lips with the speed of honey. How? How? When I am left to gather up the paper plates and the crumbs, I discover that it has been ten, twenty years...

>	her birthday party
>	long before
>		long afterwards
>	an iridescence

If it sounds like a life of wealth, it is only because, for a time, and thanks to my wife's diligence, we found a house for rent which belonged to the Department of Highways. North Hollywood was about to be split in half by a freeway and part of this jugular cut through a beautiful neighborhood to one side of the North Hollywood Park. The house we rented for some two years, for a song, began with a huge lawn in front shaded by a maple and a weeping willow and a long driveway edged with boxwood shrubs. The garden swept around to a private and very green court with its patio and its badminton and beyond that, to an orchard of lemon, apricot, peach and almond. It ended in sand, by the dry riverbed separating us from the seemingly endless forest of eucalyptus that made up the Park.

Above what was all that life, now, there is only a massive thigh of cement, and the endless roar of traffic. And so it wasn't wealth. I never had the ten cents needed to buy a cup of coffee at ten in the morning at work, when a bell announced ten minutes of grace from the grind of insurance. I never had the ten cents for the coffee in the afternoon either.

Poverty doesn't even have a chair. Quick, hurry and sit her at the head of the table. I'll go look for a bun in the obscure pantry, bumping my head, burning my hand on a hot plate left there by chance.

Across the Border I have seen poverty swim with young boys in a bile-green river not worth the names of water. And I have seen her buy ten cents worth of lard while the wind was selling papers at eye level. Poverty doesn't charge aything for her favors and she doesn't wear any undergarments. Do not, please, make the mistake of loving her more than you ought to. Poverty scares you, but once you have made her yours, you will have a slew of kids by her, and they will break their teeth on her iron teats.

> *the whole family*
> *sits down to the radishes*
> *and the saltshaker*

And the word, behind whose shape spirit took form, fearful of recognition and thus full of disguises, the word constantly about to land on our tongues, that word at last took refuge in a shape and spoke, was spoken to. It was our second son, bright, playful, shy. Our fourth and final child.

We went out hunting in New Mexico, he for the lives of sorrow, I for pebbles, small hard stones in the immemorial soil of the Rockies. And then, because he was still so tender and so tender still, we exchanged roles at the last. In one full sense at least, I shot his first bird, his first rabbit, so that he could keep the pain from being entirely his own.

He joins me to reload the gun and wonders what I am doing.

"What do you keep looking for, Dad?"

"This," I say, showing him a reddish stone, "might mean you."

The boy looks at my hand uncomprehendingly and is off after another rabbit. Another? At the end of our first stay in New Mexico, with nothing bagged, a bird landed straight ahead on the topmost branch of a berry bush.

"Kill it," I said.

The shot turned it into a fountain of feathers in the deepening light. We buried the little mess among angular bits of quartz and red earth.

On the last day of our vacation the following year we had to do away with chance.

"We'll look for three signs," I told him as we got into the car at my old friend Gene Frumkin's house and headed for the hills. Some blocks ahead the green light of an intersection beckoned. "If we make that light, it'll mean that you'll at least sight a rabbit," I said, increasing our speed. We made it on yellow. Another light, greenly beckoning at the freeway on-ramp became the second sign. We made it. That meant that he would get to shoot at a rabbit.

On the freeway I told Miguel to look at the license plate of the next car to pass us. A car passed us on the left; the letters on its plate were AH. "That's it! You'll kill your first rabbit today!"

Miguel said nothing. I don't think he believed me. We got to the hills and parked the car off the bumpy gravel road. I chose a cool spot underneath an evergreen and pulled out a book. Miguel took off. For an hour or so I heard sporadic shooting.

Had I been right? I began to feel lonely and endangered and my mood dictated the following:

> *murderers arrive*
> *see the stain on my belly*
> *and depart once more*

Then, as the sunset light waned, Miguel appeared, frustrated and spent. He had shot at several rabbits but each had had its way of avoiding extinction. There was nothing to do but go home.

Miguel unloaded the gun, I turned the car around and we began driving down the road toward the first settlements. Three hundred yards or so from the first house, as we bumped and jogged down the incline, a rabbit, sitting coolly by the side of the road, made me come to a halt.

"Load the gun and aim out the window," I told Miguel.

He wasted no time but, as we were facing the rabbit directly, there was no way he could take aim. "Open the door and slide out quietly," I said. Miguel did so. The rabbit waited, looking at us all the while. The gun went off, the rabbit leaped awkwardly in the air and disappeared into the bush.

"After him!" I shouted. "He's wounded!"

Miguel darted off after it with me following. When we caught up with the rabbit it was writhing in agony in the sand. "Kill it quickly," I whispered.

Miguel, whose face showed disbelief at the pain the creature was suffering —making it all his as I saw it— took aim and fired. Blood and guts sprayed the wild flowers all around and it was over.

There was no question of taking the small fellow home for dinner; there was hardly anything left. I cut its front left paw and gave it to Miguel. "Cure it with salt when you get back to Los Angeles," I instructed, "and put it in the sun to dry."

He did as I told him but when I asked him months later if he had his charm he told me that one of his dogs had eaten it.

"Its luck will still hold," I told him, and we never talked about it again.

> *Some may call it chance*
> *when your love waves from the hill*
> *and sees at a glance*
> *a lark in its sudden climb*
> *and a hawk poised for the kill*

Speaking of hunters, Miguel, you should have seen your grandfather at it. Not the old man you knew, holding the handkerchief to his mouth, but a younger man, lithe as a willow wand, hiding in the cold peach orchard, waiting gun in hand for the flutter of doves' wings to alight on a tree. He took to the mountains the way fog abounds in them, as beloved limbo, and he killed with pulchritude, with no swear words in the mouth; regretting, with something of Blavatsky in him, the fact that he had to eat.

Physically, he had a small head. It always presented problems when he went to buy a hat. At times we tried wads of paper inside the inner band of the hats he did buy but nothing really worked. And ever since that wasp bit him on the head when he tried to shoo it away with his hat, that time long ago when he built the dove-cote in San Antonio de Belen, he was more reverential towards the sky.

He was polite toward death and well-disposed toward men of letters. When I used to come to him, swimming across the channel of English, he would retire, yawning, into Quevedo's cave. America made him try his hand at cooking; America saw him working as a janitor, albeit not too successful a one, at an L.A. downtown jewelry store.

> *my father calls up*
> *to invite me to a plate*
> *of mondongo soup*

In his heart there was a little jasmine and a lot of oregano. Ah, when will he ever cook for me again?

> *the oregano*
> *waits patiently on the shelf*
> *till mondongo time*

What is mondongo? Ask him. Ask a cow with twenty miles or more of tripe to go before it's dark.

NOT EVEN THE FIRST BIT OF DEATH is what you expect it to be, let alone anything subsequently larger. I had just come to say goodnight to Pigo and Aglaia and had sat on Aglaia's bed when it happened. I felt nothing; something so insubstantial I did not bother to check. But I had sat on their pet, the mouse they had surreptitiously taken out of its cage and which Aglaia had under the covers.

It was only after I had kissed them and had left the room that the dead mouse was discovered. Their cries brought me and my wife into the room and it was only hours later, when they had finally fallen asleep after crying their hearts out, that I could go and throw the little death over the bridge by the railroad tracks.

Other times mice have represented different things, mostly themselves, looking as if they needed grandfatherly glasses for their noses. It is rarely that one stands out so sharply although I would have remembered its endless runs on its exercise wheel, stopping in the middle of the night only when an ambulance or the police went by with their sirens blazing.

And yet, a strangely different mouse came to me last night. I was asleep, with my mouth open, and he entered and made it his. Since then, every time I speak, something of him suffuses my words. Could it be his humility?

> *sooner or later*
> *a mouse will drown in the milk*
> *of human kindness*

When I drink water he gets wet, this mouse of intemperate hope. The mouth, you see, is the habitat of that little mouse, Humor; its home, you might say. God help the home where the bad old cat of the house has eaten the little mouse.

ALL DAY LONG THE ICICLES DRIP in the brilliant sunlight, forms gone coward. Some apples from last season cling to the tree, red with an old flush, shrunken robins that did not fly away to gravity, wrinkled and rosy like grandmothers baking the immense recipes of sugar.

It's soggy steps to the woodshed. The wind wonders when it will have something to tug at on the clothesline. That wind! That baby! Roofs with their beards wet!

There will be an everywhere of water going this way and that, nerve-endings of the river.

> *water that settles*
> *for tiny fish*
>   *could it be*
> *lullaby water?*

When the snow has melted and the sun has dried the streets and alleyways, two drunks will huddle by a warehouse door and discuss the night they have survived.

They will go down to Yakima and stand by the door of another building very much like the one on Main Street here; a building built around 1890, with the name of its original owner up somewhere by the arabesques of brick of a bygone era.

> *The flies do not know*
> *why the three fishheads are wrapped*
> *in a newspaper*
> *nameless dust has collected*
> *on each step of the staircase*

And in Yakima tonight, over by the railroad yards, they will meet other men also living as randomly, and they will drink cheap wine or whatever until their eyes become swollen and red, like the bellies of venomous spiders.

Perhaps one will die of some infallible abuse of the body, down by the river where the reeds will try to render his death as innocent as an animal's. Others will wither into fumbling decades, regulars of some Mission, really waiting for that final hand-out that will smooth all of their deep wrinkles.

Meantime, the spring will set the calendar in order. The warmth will come mounted on ponies of wind. One morning, early, with my two babies snuggled close to their mother, I will leave the sleeping town behind, with its hint of bacon in the air. I'll take the north road out, turn, pass the cemetery with its tilting tide of marble, its few fresh mounds, grassless hunchbacks of clay —for death is not yet out of style— and head for the hills that converge the light.

After the wonderful, easy, bohemian friendships of Mexico, the incipient musical career, Ellensburg is a kind of Siberia for me and fishing the only pastime that can make me forget how far away I have spun from what was once native to me.

I fish where the stream permits it, the two of us being idle and it wide, and where the trees allow the water to drink deep of shade and shadow. Berry vines put out long caterpillar arcs and wild roses bank their makeshift altars against the rocky hillside, their blossoms tough tiny epiphanies, nipples of the virginal meadow.

> *owls and wild roses*
> *the soft pink petal of dawn*
> *beaks*
>   *talons*
>   *and thorns*

One trout I never caught. He lived big under a log just before the stream took a wide turn and moved fast to keep up with a ravine. As many times as I would put a fresh salmon egg on the end of my hook, that many times he would lunch at my expense, silvery and furious when the edge of supper nicked his lip.

The little guys, under six inches, were always the most eager to surrender their lives. They came at the hook with mouths like those of fledglings in a nest, believing in the motherliness that would throw them back into the water.

...Just as you were tossed into the lively air, Pigo and Aglaia, when you were at your smallest. And you, Elena. And you too, Miguel. Hopelessly tossed from one womb into the other by irresponsible love, love that goes fishing in confused, turbulent waters...Just as your parents were tossed. In fact, we were in mid-air when we discovered that we had you to toss in the process, and get a circus-style laugh from whoever watches from the sidelines.

That period of life was, for me, a five-year exile. When I first arrived in Ellensburg, my wife was round with the first of four harvests. We didn't know exactly how we would survive. One day I dug trenches for an outfit putting up a power line through the stoniest fields in the world. That soil was so stony that the only available earth was to be found securing each rock to its neighbor. I was not used to that kind of physical work, didn't know the tricks of conserving energy. In two hours I was ready to pass out. The gang boss, who had to drive back into town, took me back with few words wasted.

Fortunately, a job opened up at the College of Education on the other side of town from where we lived. The daughter of one of our friends worked in the business office and alerted us to the fact that they were looking for a storekeeper, someone to mind the central supply room and deliver materials all over the campus. To my immense surprise I got the job, working under a somewhat dour fellow of Dutch ancestry. Most of the day I would have to hand out and make note of all the supplies that electrician, plumber, painter, carpenter and janitor required. Twice a day I had to drive a station wagon downtown with the mail and take one of the office women to the bank. In many ways it was a pleasant job, but I was not very good with the nomenclature of the million little items workmen use to fix things.

Lined up against the windows, on one side of the storeroom, there'd be five or six big metal barrels. One was soap, used by the janitors when they scrubbed the floors of their respective buildings. There was turpentine and I don't know what else in the others. The soap was a problem. When a janitor brought a gallon jug, or a five gallon container to be filled, we, either my boss or I, whoever was available at the time, would lock a dolly to the barrel, pull it down parallel to the floor, place a funnel under the spigot and begin filling the container. Since the soap had the consistency of molasses and ran out as slowly as the woes of a snail, we'd leave it running and go do other chores. That's where the trouble lay. Once in a while we'd forget only to come back later and find a lake of soap analyzing the interminable flatness of the floor. I was at fault most of the time because I was forgetful and was often called away to another building. My boss would have a fit each time although little actual soap was wasted: I'd just have to scoop it all up and pour it back into the barrel. It was quite time consuming. In revenge for his fits —the few times he'd do the same thing I'd put on this serious concerned air and go help him. That got to him in the worst way.

There were advantages to the job. I could make use of the college library and the record collection in the Music Department. I read a great deal in those days. Kafka, from the high towers of his castle, walked me home many an afternoon. The workmen would laugh at me; I reminded them of the old neighborhood priest who, on fair days, could be seen walking down the sidewalk at a snail's pace, reading his breviary.

> *he would stop and think*
> *each time he found something new*
> *in his breviary*
> *but I was just a sinner*
> *galloping through my Kafka*

Each kind of pain has its own quality. When I bump my nose, the pain is so specifically nose pain that the word pain loses some of its generic meaning when it has to be applied to, say, the feeling of very raw and chapped lips. Language is limited in that way; that is why I find it difficult to set down the modalities of my Ellensburg days: the grave nostalgia for a Mexican mariachi tune, the joy at heart over a cherry tree in bloom; or a long street with maple leaves knee deep in autumn; rivers, mountains, cliffs... the birth of one's children.

I always ask: Where is that light now? I mean the actual light that shone on such and such a day, the light that gave away the streak of yellow poplars by the river.

Pigo and Aglaia would be out in the yard, eating dirt by the handful. Even as I write this, one of them, Pigo as it happens (for he's visiting me in Minnesota) is before me. True, he is three or four times the size he was then and, instead of eating dirt he is listening to the music of Satie. But he is the essence of what he was then. What other possibility for survival did all that sunshine have, on the other hand? Its tenderness, its infinitely mysterious gift, was to be seemingly insubstantial and yet totally indispensible. It fed the soul its banquet of visibilities, to mention only the obvious. It anchored us and became our process...

To find one's way back to life is to go back to its light, to its dust in the soul, and ask it to speak.

The first house we lived in belonged to my wife's family. It was on South Main, a few blocks before the cattails announced the end of town. In front there were two young trees, a catalpa and a willow, each one struggling for hegemony. On warm afternoons, Pigo would be waiting for me on the front porch, strapped to his bouncing metal chair.

> *once you start to jump*
> *the catalpa understands*
> *another willow*

In back, my brother-in-law's strawberry patch grew to one side of the weathered out-house, seat of summer philosophy and winter hurry. The world seemed balanced between beauty and necessity.

> *day of reckoning*
> *I retreat to the toilet*
> *Jonah to the whale*

The house was nothing more than a large cabin. My brother-in-law occupied one room and we the other. In the kitchen a wood stove made sure that ice wasn't part of the menu. When it got going it put out tremendous amounts of heat; it always surprised me that the flimsy walls did not go up in a blaze of glory. In that small room things could get so hot one couldn't touch the walls (at least, I remember it being so). A pigeon wing was used to sweep the top of the stove clean since the burning of wood created some cinders and dirt. It was the stove's wisk broom, but with a mate somewhere else in the universe, probably no longer recognizable as mate, a thing disassembled and torn. The use of such a wing was no doubt a folk custom in rural America. It would fill me with sadness, that stiff wing; or rather, its new function, so completely different from the function to which the previous owner had put it to in clear air. But I used it also to get to know what it must be like to be a bird. I would hold it and test its various strengths. The long end feathers had a resilience that made that wing a perfect thing to sweep crumbs and dust off the stove. The enjambment of disparate functions made it seem less surreal.

Its cartilage, of course, had long before gone hard as bird bone and so the wing as a whole had an open, frozen gesture, like the faces of certain old women behind orthodoxy. But the other feathers, curving defensively over dismal calcium gave back to softness what it must have had in its heyday.

The beauty of pigeons has always appealed to me. One can't ever compare them to more numinous birds, nor engage in the gossip of their detractors, those who claim that pigeons are dumb. They hew to some Chinese Middle of the Road and if they have any appeal it will have to be their very pigeonness. In Los Angeles once, traveling through Downtown on a bus on my way to work, I saw this girl, part of a group of people waiting for a bus. At her feet pigeons pretended that the sidewalk was their natural habitat; they went about the process of looking for crumbs:

> *the Japanese girl*
> *lets one of the white pigeons*
> *walk between her legs*

I had to order the poisoned grain that the short, ruddy janitor of the Administration Building fed the pigeons messing the outside walls of his building with their droppings. People mix a weird sense of the aesthetic with their denial of the flesh and so the lives of these eternally cooing animals had to be snuffed out so that a pile of bricks should remain spotless. How beautiful it would have been if the art students ensconsed on the second floor had protested the killing. They had no way of knowing in advance that such a thing was being planned but I doubt if any of them would have related the act of creation with the act of preservation. People concentrate on one thing to the exclusion of others. Who knows if they missed the cooing, preoccupied as they were with learning the process of silk-screening —so new then— or if song meant no more than silence to their visually-oriented minds. And who am I to raise such issues? I only complained to one or two persons and then looked the other way when a dead pigeon called up to me from the spot where it had fallen.

FOUR THOUSAND MILES SOUTH, as memory flies, if you go for a walk in the country, it is possible that some peasant might sell you a bit of honey, or moonshine if he knows you, or chirimoyas. And that he will talk of the coming rains, one foot on the barbed wire fence.

But then again, he may be out of any or all of these things, in which case you might hear the unseen wife call out from the house.

>   *we're out of honey*
>   *tell the blue-eyed customer*
>   *we're out of honey*

And ah, the comfort of being among one's own, of knowing the littlest facial quirk of the language, there where meaning and old age plant their crows' feet together.

I was born in the country that smiles the most, in the country of the smile with which a mother greets the thing she holds in her arms. It is only later that one comes to the world. First comes feast, family, not a single poker face for miles around. And the Church!

Nothing like the Church to keep you and your grandmother busy. Even in its cunning decrepitude the Church is charming, and the easiest thing to shed when you decide to grow up and give up childish ways. On the other hand, who can imagine a Marxist family proper? Praying to Lenin when there is an earthquake? Cursing the capitalist war dogs when bad news comes surgery-way? Listen comrades, only faith can keep you, me, anyone, honest. Didn't you know that about yourselves? Ah, you didn't want to hear it! You are trying to do away with the mystery, hack away at it with logic, with reason. Good luck! As for me, the most beautiful thing in the world is what has to do with faith; even its lack, if come to with humility.

Only those who turn their backs completely on faith can be exploiters. And if you argue that faith is wrong precisely because tyrants take advantage of those who have it, —to that I say that faith is so benign and open that it allows itself to be misused.

What faith does is mask a style of passage, be it blind another way. Faith is almost as noble as forgiving. And you might need it for that.

Your name, Antonio; your names, Josefina and Guadalupe; your assignations at the courthouse, your prerogatives of a baptismal fire, your indumenta at the hour of seals and fervent prayer, your names will rattle like thunder on the pure shingle of the grave and tumble head-first into the pit with you.

From time to time, to mark the quarter centuries, someone with the yellowed fingers of nicotine will shuffle through the silt of paper in some abandonable office and detect, in passing, that the very ribbons with which they tied your provincial rights have now crumbled into dust. And what can you do but blow upon the numb trumpets of your hands throughout that winter? The melting bodies of your names shall be called out in succession by the moist and varying light of summertime; by that flood that, shoving all stone aside, will buoy and render you high and dissolute.

Back home your niece will place roses and geraniums by your photograph, your mother will have a rosary said. The wafting will continue. One movement, one arm of nature smuggles you to unknown, disfigured safety.

From the house on main street, when my job at the college seemed secure, we moved to a court around the corner from the Maintenance Building where I worked. Cottonwood trees shimmered blond in the autumn air. Aglaia, you were born shortly before we moved there, and from the bedroom where you slept so much in waking to life, one could hear the small brook that ran behind the court, mainly a gossiping of stone and water, gravity tilted toward distance. Was it that brook that lent you the voice with which you sing a Mitchell song so beautifully?

We moved to give my brother-in-law room to live his life. He had found himself a girlfriend; was almost happy then, this tough steelworker with a yen for alcohol.

That fall everything turned unbelievably crisp and golden. The days held their breath as if to test how long the trees could cling to their metallic hair-do's. From the large windows of my storeroom I caught sparrows at play one sunny afternoon. A row of medium-sized trees with large leaves lined the street. These trees, you could sense it, could barely hang on another hour to their treasures; they were pitchers of beer filled to the brim. A crowd of sparrows, a goodly one, no less mischievous than school children, descended on the richest tree of the lot and, chirping their hearts out, laughing their fool heads off, proceeded to leap and leap and leap from one branch, from one twig, to another. The bath began; it was a shower of leaves crinkling and clanking and turning in air, corruscating the ground with gold leaf until the entire tree was bare, naked for winter. Then the sparrows flew away; they had had enough. Did they take count to see who among them had loosened the most leaves? Feverish gamesters! How I loved their taking time out from their ominously fast metabolism in order to play!

I had opened the big delivery door quietly to see them better from where I had to work, and to hear the rumpus they were raising. Something about their crazy innocence made a dent in my heart; they were the most carefree cup of laughter offered to me alone at that time, in that place.

>*how many sparrows*
>*can take a bath in the gold*
>*of a single tree?*

Up the next street, a smallish mountain ash, with its clusters of orange berries, did not lose its fruit when the snows began falling. One day I passed in front of it and what I saw were some fifty small red faces each one topped by a cone of snow for a hat. To me these are visions; what I love about them is their significance, devoid of overtones. There is no symbology; no human purpose can be ascribed to them. They happen because the entire cosmos dwells on surprise, a mineral, vegetal and animal bliss illuminating existence.

>*sparrows in the yard*
>*the snow has come and caught them*
>*without their sweaters*

In that court we made the acquaintance of many people. They return now, the ones indelible for whatever chance reason, who lived side by side with us and with forgotten shadows: the small Protestant minister and his equally small wife, old and wrinkled like happy raisins. He worked with the painting crew at the college, an uncomplaining victim of secularism. Then there was the pretty wife of the fellow in charge of Visual Aids, perennially pushing a pram with a new baby in the wake of their happiness. And a couple of Swedish descent; he a professor of physics at the college and a vacuum cleaner salesman on the side; she busy with two children and her inconsolable menopause.

One summer there, while the wind turned the volume up in the cottonwoods, I read Conan Doyle in my leisure hours. Ever since, the romance of intelligence versus crime is inseparable from the rub of young air against porous towers of green.

> *I don't have a clue*
> *twenty*
> *thirty years of wind*
> *and the sound so fresh*

There is in the wind the sound of what it touches and then, a bit afterwards, the distance, often of itself, often of a silence in the shape of an infinite caress that progresses through dawn, through light, through evening, staining nothing, passing. The wind is a body of wants without want, going nowhere, somewhere, without us, and in the end, everywhere without us, a handsome thing for the earth to be crowned with, a pure thing with us or without.

SCHOOL! SCHOOL! I STILL REMEMBER the very tone of the school bell ringing for recess. It seemed to split the school in half like a pomegranate. We seed would spill into the park, hungry and eager, young and ready, the park where green shadows rose fifty feet into the air and otherwise put eternity to sleep. A nickel would burn its way through the pocket of want and the peddlers of peanuts, candy and icecream would develop octopal abilities until the next bell, a bell that would drain the park of life so that silence, with its flamingo legs, could stalk the inner hammers of the ear.

> *a leaf drops near him*
> *the startled icecream vendor*
> *lets go with his cry*

It was a day so young I had a father with a father, a time so green my mother had her mother with her. I came home to the gift. It was a belt I needed, the belt I wore all through childhood and up. Eventually, the belt itself wore out and the buckle went on to fit a longer strap of waistline. But it, too, eventually showed signs of age, scratches and the mark of the tongue that went through the eye of the leather and rubbed against the main bar of the buckle.

> *how it hurts to see*
> *the work of time in a thing*
> *like a belt buckle*

Years later, when I inherited my great-grandfather's guitar, what should have scratched its back in a wide arc but his belt buckle! I had it redone, it needing glue and love, and now Aglaia plays it and her voice, which is the lacework of ten mountains, resonates in its cave.

Around 1937, children, when I was not a father but a child myself, we were poor enough to be lucky and live at my grandmother's house. There, every family section had a room to itself and some of the single persons doubled up. It was a house filled to the brim with the various shapes of love, old folks whose souls knew of no wrinkles, perfect loaves of evening bread, then younger ones with various jobs and children plus two or three servants who cleaned, ran errands and filled the place with the mystical odor of saffron in the cooking rice. It must be remembered that servants worked for practically nothing, the chance to eat three meals a day and have a roof over their heads; and that kitchen work in those days was not automated: you had to go to the store each day to buy the perishable items. Cooking itself was a long and laborious task. Having three servants was not a sign of wealth at all; it made living possible.

My childhood, like a shiny toy, is hoisted and delivered, wearing the engine-red of a lady-bug. Old folk —those incipient shadows— made it sure and rich. Those ancient cronies, pushing seventy and eighty, warm, orange-peeling, story-telling, penny-wise, bed-tucking worthies! Neine, Pachico (the grandmother whom I called Pinto), Quetica, Atún (Grand-uncle Tuna)...

Their life-long servant Leocadia is frying chips of green plantain and the pan is a concerto of mixed-up crickets.

> *these words*
> *somehow yours*
> *now that I've opened my trap*
> *to say good morning*

What am I doing in the kitchen? "Out! Do you hear? Out!" Leocadia has not time for a mere boy. She is a busy person and won't pay any attention to me until I return to my homeland with a wife. Eleven, twelve years have passed. Most of the old folks are gone and she, Neine and my aunt Edna live across the hall from us in an apartment building sublet by my enterprising aunt Aida.

Leocadia now takes it upon herself to bring us our breakfast each morning. Of the two haiku I have written about it I prefer this one:

> *something of a task*
> *to wake up the newlyweds*
> *with breakfast at eight*

because it portrays her nature best, a reserved quality of mischievous elegance (the Latin-American middle classes do not understand a word of this) which would make me smile and which would bring to mind Lenin's dictum, that the task of the revolution is to see that cooks learn to govern the world. As if they didn't.

On the other hand, the other haiku tells more of the story:

> *her coffee with cream*
> *only newlyweds can sleep*
> *after she brews it*

Her coffee was incredible, and she'd bring it with that funny mini-smile to one side of her face, with toast and guava jelly.

Guavas, loquats... the after-school feast on the breast of a meadow, before the inevitable downpour of the afternoon.

> *a single raindrop*
> *I am myself that someone*
> *a shout brought running*

Childhood is like that, a matter of shouts, of dinners getting cold, of smoothly flowing water, depth. You peek in and see yourself beribbonned by cloud; you see pebbles, a face, and someone stealing the pie. When the surface undulates, the thief is far away.

Has he hidden, perhaps, in our farm in San Antonio? In that village of humdrum adobe, heavy-bellied houses pregnant with hospitality? In that church with its air of ruptured sweetness?

Across the river, with the eye needing no spider's bridge, that long hill stretches with the consistency of a girl's thigh. Good days bathe it in cloud and light, and the rain bathes it green.

There is a well of green to the source of vegetation, a stable in the mountains held up by the thread of a star, which you can find by following the shoestring of a road. It is a stable of mist and brothers, a stable of the flow of love, the lowing of kindness, with a heart like the pip of a green peach.

Time we found it again. Time we went back and searched for its foundations. The wind pounces on the breeze, suddenly; it falls upon its unsuspecting petal with a triton's laugh, the older brother's silver prank.

Of course, I am talking about San Antonio de Belen. Where the train arrives panting for breath because, in going down toward the sea, it has to brake itself, its lust for gravity... A long curve, a skinny bikini bridge, built by a tipsy tight rope walker, and it arrives at the station, a trail of inept chicken squawks behind it and —once— that slaughtered pig...

The heat is already that of rose apples, empty-handed, like the sex of angels. It is the heat of the Pacific, not so far away, and it is also like a straight road no one traverses without a whistled tune.

In the town each merchant is a barrel of sarsaparilla. A few seagulls enter the front of the church for the holy water in the stone offertory, salty from many fingers. How is it that life is not the year before's? The smile of chance.

> *dear thief*
> *the gulls drink*
> *from the stone offertories*
> *salty with your tears*

Is time really such a good thief? As we get older life becomes more cautious but still open. Indeed, some of the doors are still banging. When we had the big house on Lemp, with its orchard and the park behind, beyond, one day a bum ventured in among the trees and stood hesitantly there. I went out to see what he wanted. He wanted food. I went back to the house, searched, found nothing suitable, went out and gave him fifty cents instead.

How do I know what he really wanted? He wanted food. Food? All theft is property.

Now, if one were to return to San Antonio at night, walking across the fields and hoping that there is nothing more to nature than what one knows of it already, nothing more to shadows than what one squashes with dawn, with what relief would one sight the house in the distance! Even at the risk of stepping into the wrong thing:

> *it's just a candle*
> *a candle in the window*
> *(bootful of cowdung)*

And is it a candle?

> *there it is again*
> *a firefly deep in love*
> *with a falling star*

In San Isidro the nights are so dark that they are purple, each one a half-opened package under the arm of the woebegone moon, hitchhiking without experience down the lonely highway of the sky. The eye of the firefly burns with desire and then, moments later...

> *the fog comes and writes*
> *its own enormous poem*
> *with its eraser*

MIGUEL COMES OUT TO THE GARDEN, a moustache of milk stamped over a smile of satisfaction.

"Hey, help me with this rock!" I ask my tiny Atlas.

He drinks milk as if it were water, perhaps because it resembles it so much nowadays. But it wasn't so long ago that milk came thumbs down for the juice, thumbs up for cream, and you could tell the potency of the stuff by the amount of the latter in each of the proud and sweaty bottles on the porch.

> *how absurd of God*
> *on the neck of the bottle*
> *a cravat of silk*

Not any more. Milk, like life itself, is homogenized, homosapienized, and only in sleep does the hairdresser dream of setting the mane of a lion ablaze with sunsets.

Do you want another small fable, Miguel? This one will fit in your shirt pocket:

The compassionate revolution comes and there is a general feeling of deliverance. Fences are torn down and trampled underfoot; walls, compartments and frontiers are exiled into history. To our surprise, the animals join us. In a burst of enthusiasm they learn to speak. Some of them tell us what it was like under the old regime:

> *one of her nipples*
> *was for Mother Superior*
> *that's what the cow says*

TO: Dad

I know that you don't believe in Fathers day or any religious thing. I am getting you this gift because I love you, I know you will enjoy this.

Love: Miguel Cardenatine

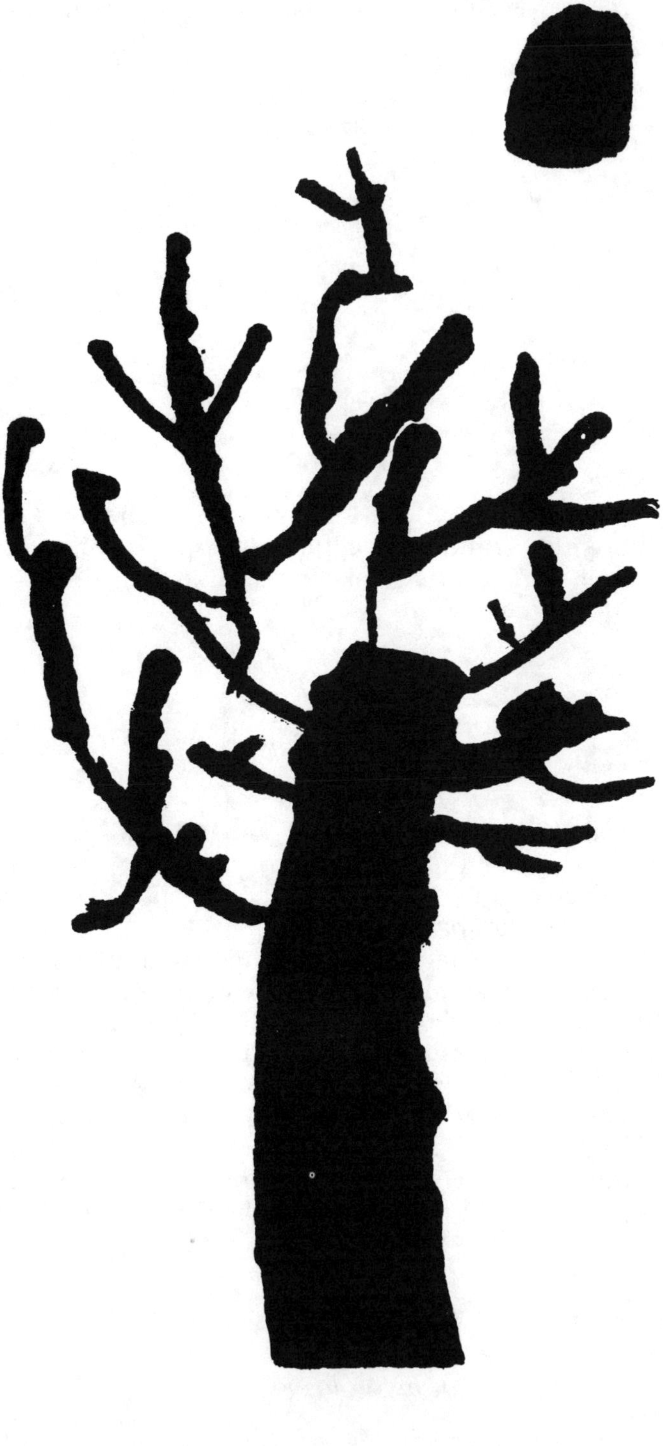

Listen, even the heavenly bodies are on the side of cattle:

>*well*
>>*what do you know*
>*four horns on the sleeping cow*
>*shoo*
>>*shoo*
>>>*crescent moon*

BUT NOW, AGLAIA AND PIGO, LET US say goodbye to Campus Courts. You, Aglaia, cannot remember what a pretty baby you were. One time I put you on your blanket on the floor of the living room so that I could take a picture.

>*Aglaia*
>>*look here*
>*look at me*
>>*look at yourself*
>*in my direction*

The picture must still be around somewhere —your mother must have it— but not the you you were, wiggling your arms and legs like a ladybug on her back before she catapults herself back to normalcy with her carapace.

Pigo, you, being a year older, might remember the rocking horse I made for you, shiny and bright-eyed, to the surprise of people — my boss for one— who thought I was all thumbs.

Rocking horses sometimes forget that they are under oath not to reveal any secrets about their deities, horses with wings and horses with horns. When they tell children —when they cannot help themselves out of love— the fables become real and they and the children riding them are suddenly transformed into centaurs.

But Pigo, you'll have to excuse me. When I tried to write a good haiku only a topsy-turvy one came out, with its seven syllables up front!

>*the unicorn unscrews it*
>*and dumps out an air*
>*of mythology*

That's the way that kind come, the topsy-turvy ones. Myth leads to imperfect haiku, though it might fit the form. I cannot see myths as anything but crutches; when a poet's jaw is weak he or she uses myth to prop it up.

This next one, however, casts no shadow;

> *a herd of horses*
> *fording the moonlit river*
> *oh hidden centaur*

When my mother and father came visiting they helped us buy a house that had more than one bedroom to its name. In fact, it came with a duplex to one side and they and my sister with her two children by her first marriage lived there for a time.

We would cook a large pot of spaghetti, invite my friend John, and drink enough wine to forget the weather and the latitude. I had met John at the cannery during one summer when I used my two week vacation at the college to earn some extra money. The corn would come in, green tons of it, and everyone in town would pitch in and work in relays around the clock.

One night, just as I was coming in with my shift, I looked over and there was this nice fellow in huge rubber boots, hosing down the machinery. Something made me go over and start a conversation. Sure enough, a friend from the first! I have a knack for finding key friends in the most obscure places.

The fact that, one or two years later, John abandoned us for Scotland one fine day doesn't matter in the least. He left us the memory of his rich laugh, the echo of that endless hunt for a home that men who love philosophy or sail the seas seem to have in common. We shared music, fishing, endless talk. Together we went to Seattle, where his friend George introduced me to bonsai and Indian music...

> *this is the earth*
>   *friends*
> *a place of shadows and love*
> *without a shadow*

We would laugh at you, Pigo, prancing around with a tin horn from an old-fashioned victrola, imitating the orchestral sounds of Revueltas or Bartok, a baby about to go to bed and dream rainbows of sound...

> *he won't go to sleep*
> *unless we play him the tune*
> *that keeps him awake*

10th Street was on the edge of town, above everything; close, it seemed, to the source of the endless cold wind that blew in the spring. The Cascade Mountains loomed white in the distance, the teeth of a giant bulldog trying to bite a hunk of heaven. Even so, the most delicate things were able to thrive in that atmosphere: cherry, apple and pear blossoms, the unassuming lilac with its fragrance of bodies forever young, icicles on sunny days refracting light into a blinding grammar of color.

The sunlight is there. And the grass it has only syllabically begun to resemble. And the wind which shuffles past it, we don't know how. Only the sunlight speaks, and the wind is the space between its teeth, the word *yes* pronounced in all the simultaneous languages of time. The soil, so dark, so evangelical, turns that *yes* into a verb between its compact fingers and that *yes* blooms. Blooming implies flight, the banishing of walls, a good trembling.

> *like myself*
> *like me*
> *nameless flowers everywhere*
> *without destiny*

The dream function is a tangent of energy that oversteps the ego. Is it any wonder that pillows resemble clouds?

Every afternoon, after work, I had to bring in the wood for the central stove that kept us warm. The cord of wood neatly stacked against the garage wall would suffer the loss of a few armfuls, and the path between it and the house would be lined with chips and pieces of bark dropped on the way. The most exciting part of stacking the wood after it was dumped in the alley was finding the pieces of pitch that would make lighting the stove so easy. But the work of hauling in the wood each day all winter long was a drudge.

Spring meant freedom. Liberation into length as well, with the days getting longer, handsomer, and the children on longer outings. Aglaia took to wandering off; one time we found her three blocks away. But how can one be angry with a child who sees the whole world as home? They learn to walk so gingerly, to be erect as trees. All of my children were walking by the time they were eight months old, which must be some kind of a record. Aglaia, where is that first pair of white leather shoes we got for you when you were on the verge of walking?

> *shoes so dear to me*
> *they all but take a few steps*
> *in my direction*

But children, avoid your parents, they are pessimists who know that childhood doesn't last.

SPRING SURPRISES NO ONE. HOW COULD IT? We often pinch ourselves to recall the fact that we are alive. When it hurts we smile and check the season. If it is spring, we are surprised.

But summer! Summer surprises even the dead, it catches them on its horns and tosses them skyward, like those drunks who enter the bullring at Christmas time in Costa Rica and end up nursing broken ribs. The dead in summer enter their time of zymurgy; at midnight, the cemeteries turn into swamps of high hope.

But pinch or no, our lives are going down the drain so we'd better hurry and take a last look around, we who somehow find the *now* so inadequate, wallowing in the freedom to be imperfect.

> *God says* universe
> *and the universe replies*
> *in pidgin English*

IN SAN ANTONIO YOU CROSSED A WOODEN bridge, roused the chickens or a dog, and you were in the house of my father's friend, the town's electrician. His ghosts —for he told ghost stories to scare us kids— were electrical misconducts, thyroid shorts of disproportionate strength. There were nights when I could not sleep, worrying over the headless figure that lunges at travelers when they are crossing a bridge.

If you were in the house of the electrician, you did not point your wooden toy at their somewhat wooden souls, for they had carved their souls' awareness out of vegetal divinities, and the nodule where a branch had pushed its way into sky might be the umbilical tattoo, forerunner of taboos.

Ring! Ring! Touch the belly button of noise, of children, of brooms, of the flowers of mica, of the fields where a certain season proves best. What to do but play with his girl and boy in their torn clothes? The distance between us is a triangular caress, a hidden sharing of cheese, a migraine of bulls. It is also a subtle and most ancient odor of anger, of which we children know nothing as yet. As children we simply embroider Sunday into the skirts of the week, jointly we put up the cuffs of Friday. We definitely do not know the meaning of those railroad tracks separating our separate houses.

> *armpit and navel*
> *beyond the railroad tracks grow*
> *flowers of insight*

San Antonio is best when the rest of the family comes visiting. A busload and the house is full. Three feet of adobe wall feel thinner thanks to company, to those random hammocks of talk, smiles of hemp from oak rafter to rafter.

In each bedroom, squared off crocodiles, gourmands of clothes, are unpacked and, while the cousins explore the four cornerstones of the farm, the corners of each bed are turned down for a noon-time peek at the ripening harvest of sleep. The sky predicates blue and hopes that the sun won't singe its rimless wonder. Hunger, which had stalked the scarecrow until now, insists on salivation, a table groans under a tree.

Suspicious birds, guarding their nests at the Y's of that tree, look down with lavished eye. But all that goes on, finally, is a sharing, a pass-me-this-and-a-little-more-of-that, while the napkins, conscious of their-not-too-prosperous cousins, the handkerchiefs, politely limit their scurrying to the overstuffed mouth.

Talk darns a sock that needed darning. We children lie in the tall grass and count clouds or the clouds pile up and count children hurrying for cover. San Antonio de Belen, a town of rare clay, of gagging sunlight, half way down to the burning sea, lapped by its warm breeze, its sotto voce lips, its senseless hands!

The sometimes otherwise: the train goes by, the last bus and... nothing! They didn't come. Eddies of dust, caught off balance, stop spinning and disintegrate. Marvelous fossils, half-buried in the trunks of trees, invent their own gigantic aches.

The clocks finally and irrevocably wind down; their odor hides under the armpit...

> *does anyone know
> where the clock gets the notion
> that it tells the time?*

A scorpion bite, an illness; something kept them in the city, aunts, grandmothers, cousins. So Saturday goes; each day brings its own funnel, its own hood of bright gold wool that turns blue-black with holes in it.

And Sunday at dawn, with the peasants of the household, the up-at-five-o'clock servants: it's off to Mass.

Three buttons to the shirt, bend down and pull your pants on, up, find the right shoe for the left foot, the one diminishing with toes, tie it and run, be stopped in the kitchen, blessed in one gulp... and go, the strain of a comb on your matted hair felt by the rooster outside. There's the lucidity of the night-long dew upon the land while the day tries on its strength casually, exuberantly, each of its meals a button quelling a riot of fingers. The river tries on its pair of pants, finding them long, running away with the measurements...

Inside the church everyone's so still, so into the tug of grace and mystery, the necessary remedy to life; there are people praying so earnestly, so fervently, that one cannot stand too close to them without feeling feverish in turn. And there are lips formulating the powers of saints and the hands of the drowning clasped around the straw of salvation.

> *each single peasant
> has already passed with ease
> through the needle's eye*

You are the pubic absence of a forest, a phoneme of silence waiting to turn into careless shouts later with your friends, the policy of youth, bone and leap grabbing the beehive, the hornet's nest, to run with it like a football, chased by the chase, by a component rind of animal indignation...

Yes, I was so much a child, children, that you surprise me separate!

Now we're in the garden, and while the wife worries over the ajuga, sunlight threads the needles of the pine with the sap of summer. How we love the shade! How we want a private hum to envelop us, to surround this house of ours. Who would have thought North Hollywood would be like this? When we're not looking

> *a snail glides over*
> *the numberless openings*
> *of the honeycomb*

One day it is all finished: the rock converses with the bamboo, a hummingbird invents the icon of a flower and hovers in front of it, saying its pater noster of nectar... The garden is finished. And the snails?

> *the snails*
>   *oh my God*
> *they get erections of light*
> *with those eyes of theirs*

How did we do it? By counting the chlorophyl of each syllable. A Japanese garden is a private moment in the breath of orchestration: silent branches move their shadows over the contour of the ground, the rocks signal to one another, wishing there were tiny clouds with which they could communicate better, the way mountains do...
By coincidence, we met a well-to-do Chicano who made sandals and who owned a shady acre around his old-style house in the Valley. He was on his way out, having sold his place to a company that would raze his oasis and build an apartment complex on the site (alas, leaving only one lone palm tree in memory of his overgrown paradise). Years before, he had purchased some rather magnificent rocks in Utah. These rocks were formed by succeeding bands of blues and greys, often striated: one softer and indented, the next one harder, prominent. These layers curved and shifted with the capriciousness of wind markings on sand. Our acquaintance had used a large number of these rocks in bad taste to build a sunken barbeque pit but many others lay half-buried throughout his yard. He was totally agreeable to our taking whatever plants and rocks we could carry away and my wife and I turned into ants, every day carting loads back to our house.

All that lifting injured my back so that to this day I am lucky if I see twenty-four hours go by without pain. At the time I was unaware of the danger and much too involved with the realization of our plans to stop and worry about it. I had good plans; and in actuality, the garden turned out more beautiful than I had expected. Instead of a lawn with a single tree's dandruff all year long we now had a shimmer of bamboo shutting off the street and neighbors, young pines reaching for the sky, mounds buttressed with exquisite rocks, held in place with ajuga and moss.

> *a few shovelfuls*
> *in this world of illusion*
> *and you have mountains*

But the children are not confused about color. They don't use color to describe things but to tell us how they feel about them. The stallion we saw light blue in its stunning meadow by Las Virgenes Canyon becomes, by dint of the strong thumbprint of passion from hours of impatience, the crayon of home.

> *he's actually blue*
> *the stallion that the children*
> *have painted purple*

That should remind us that the perfection of dogma is the only thing that must be wrong to be right.

EVENTUALLY, THINGS AT THE COLLEGE IN ELLENSBURG went sour for me. A new plant manager was hired after a tall, skinny, silent man with a ghostly smile had left the post vacant. The new one was a beef-eater. And for the first time, he was also directly over me.

This Mr. Beef-eater disliked me from the first and being a petty and conniving sort of man, he enjoyed setting one employee against another. Soon, he had currents of animosity blowing down the hallways of the plant. He encouraged his favorites to bitch about everything and these fellows criticized me behind my back. He set out to get rid of me.

For that he claimed that I was no good as Store Manager, my recent position. He proposed placing me with the two plumbers as assistant, assuming that I would not accept this step down. But I had no choice. And since I knew nothing about plumbing I just tagged along with one or the other of them, unplugging drains and changing faucets and kicking the washing machines back into action. Of the two plumbers, Tom, fat and impatient, was a pain in the ass. If he had to go down a man-hole I had to stand directly above it and keep a watch in case he had his impending heart attack. He was horrified of having an attack while out of sight and would fly into a towering rage if I moved the slightest distance away.

Every worker is different, he handles tools and materials differently. I got so that, walking into the plumbing shop, I could tell which of the two men had been there last and for what reason. Such knowledge!

> *the plumber is out*
> *I turn to his monkey-wrench*
> *for information*

When Mr. Beef-eater's ploy did not work and it looked as if the plumbers did not hate my guts, he shoved me onto the garden crew. Surely, —he must have thought,— now he'll quit. But my situation was desperate, there was no other place in that small town where I could have obtained a job. A job doing what? I had to cling to what I had by hook or crook.

Something else was also taking place at the same time; something of enormous importance for me and my whole future development. I had grown increasingly unhappy with my philosophical stance. Reality was speaking to me with voices that I could not interpret and it was time that I look into my satchel, throw out what wasn't needed and travel on with a lighter burden.

Since the age of fifteen, when I had turned to a very utopian Marxism as the solution to all the world's ills with the passion that only a young person possesses, the world and its wants had turned many a corner. Mankind had had its legs severed and I was standing in front of it with a band-aid in my hand. That band-aid went far back into my childhood. The roots of my supposed dialectical materialism had to do with the family I was born into. From my father's side I had inherited a strong anti-clerical bias. My grandfather had written a novel exposing the moral corruption of the Latin-American priesthood. My father, on the one hand a politically enlightened person and, on the other, a man fascinated by the esoteric doctrines of his brother Rafael, had always been militantly anti-Catholic even though he had allowed my mother to raise his children in the Church. With the Spanish Civil War there came a sharpening of the ideological conflict between Church and the needs of large masses of dispossesed people in the Spanish world (the Church, stupidly, had continued to be the spokesman for the status quo). I recall getting into fistfights at school over Spain.

Later, during World War II, I read the Red Dean of Canterbury's glowing accounts of life in Russia. To my impressionable mind, it seemed as if Paradise was just around the corner... if only the people got to own the means of production!

All through my twenties, however, life taught me something else. Being obdurate, it took me years to see the point of the lesson; many things had to coalesce before I could think for myself and therefore act differently. What I kept having to face became excruciatingly clear in the light of Zen Buddhism: that things and events are superbly what we make them, that my take on reality was just that, a take; that abstraction (and political thought is the supreme abstraction) is the cold blade that cuts through history brutalizing men. By abstraction I mean idea, nothing less. Human beings are enamoured of ideas, they are encouraged by teachers to espouse them without ever giving thought to how and when they become their slaves.

Of course, Zen did not come to save me; it came precisely when I was ready to understand its meaning. If I had run into it before I was ready for it I would have called it sheer obscurantism. But in many ways, the longer I lived the more unhappy I was with my old set of ideas; they were like a straightjacket hampering the movement of my soul. The poetry that kept emerging from me was subjective, lyrical; nothing that one could reconcile with any party line.

My reading turned much more eclectic and I began to feel a strange attraction for religious writings, not the orthodox stuff but that which was patently and unashamedly mystical, from the hibiscus of the Hindus to the little flowers of St. Francis. A crisis was building up, grounded on my inability to break out of a thought-imposed construct on reality. Then two things happened, two things in a sense unrelated yet deeply the same. One day, one of the plumbers and I had to crawl under the Science Building in order to fix something or other. In the semi-darkness of that nether space I saw objects that had been left there and forgotten by everyone: bricks, dust, cobwebs for curtains on the few small windows just above ground level. Those things struck me as being as far away from a divine plan as I was or felt to be. And I wondered how that could be. My subjective state of want had found a perfect counterpart in that crawl space. To see those materials waiting for some future sort of deliverance, for a place in the sun, as the saying goes, made my own condition obvious: it was just impossible to be outside an over-all grace I sensed permeating everything. This grace, which had been laying siege to my heart, coming closer and closer, was suddenly there. That total absence of charm, of warmth, in that dark and dreary place, and my acute sense of discomfort face to face with it, were only apparent. The grace was there and by looking for it I became aware that no looking was necessary. Every speck of dust and mortar was humming with perfect, solitary happiness.

A strange elation overcame me. I said nothing to my companion; he would not have understood. All I knew was that something extremely important had happened to me, in me.

Many times, during the following weeks, I went back to that crawl space in my mind. Those objects were etched clearly in my mind's eye as brothers in want and permanence. They really comforted me. They were things despised, abandoned and yet strangely at ease, not hankering after a better state, more sunlight, a real use. Their composite patience, their surrender to the unmoving heart of time, took me out of the human dilemma that was my problem, the foisting of a mental construct on things, people and events. I recalled the cobwebs, perfectly abandoned by their makers, and how they sagged, pregnant with dust. The beauty of their curving! The bricks, strewn about in an overwhelmingly random order-disorder fashion! Rejected wooden boards, curling from age back into tree inclinations! Shapes of tin and other metals, in tense dialogue with their never striving for the tension...!

I don't recall how long afterwards I was walking home one noon hour for lunch when, suddenly, it came to me at gut level that whether I believed that God existed or not did not matter in the least as far as His actual existence or non-existence was concerned. What was *was*!

An immense relief, after years of a basic and gritty nihilism, flooded through me. I nearly floated the rest of the way home. My true life was about to start and it was grounded on total acceptance of the fact that my mind was never going to comprehend or even perceive realities stacked miles high in the magic storehouse of time and space, realities shifting in modality with the very energy that attempted to perceive them. In fact, my mind was the obstacle; it was a marvelous tool for helping me across the street, for building a bridge. But it could never, would never understand a single fundamental *why*. Why indeed are we here? Why is there something instead of nothing?

That experience took place on a very fine day when the sky was filled with sunlight. Although I didn't realize it at the time, it was a gift the very opposite from the one before. What took place this time was almost totally internal and not a reaction to my surroundings. And yet my surroundings were now gloriously beautiful instead of being dismal by men's standards!

Many years had to go by before the consequence of those insights began to show in my life. For a time I even thought that my task would be to find a philosophical bridge between materialism and this mystical ground. I tried, but in practice what began to take place was a growing impatience with programs, with that simplistic assumption —part of all political viewpoints— that says that "we" can affect change and that "we," as opposed to "they," know what is needed.

As if one door were the friend of another, I was allowed to grow in a direction filled with superb surprises. Haiku and Zen, Indian music, things perfumed by an ancient docility and wisdom came my way, made sense and became mine.

In spite of the aggravations at work —which, together with a poor diet led to a stomach ulcer— this period was a time of almost pure acceptance for me. Kafka was unlimited absence, Tolstoy was idiot love. The garden crew was made up of a kindly foreman, a very decent man, and a few old codgers, garden desperados with whom I got along well.

> *autumn's here again*
> *the trees they blush they undress*
> *chaste*
>   *obedient*
>   *cold*

For days, weeks, I stood deep in leaves, raking, raking. My hands had callouses and my heart was singing a crazy song. It had discovered how fluid joy is; that it doesn't depend on any internal or external conditions, illness or death; that no viscissitude can touch it nor time-lapse dim its hidden, obvious smile.

The plant manager didn't know what to do. I was like one of those pieces of chewing gum stuck to one's shoe: no way to get rid of it. So one day he just flew into a rage and for an hour raved at me furiously, baiting me as best he could, exaggerating everything he could. I was struck dumb by this show of volcanic violence, and his secretary —for this took place in his office— just sat there with her mouth open.

At the end of the hour I slunk away. The few attempts I made to contradict him only made him angrier so that I ended up taking his diatribe in silence.

That same day I took a gamble. I went and knocked on the door of the college president's office. His secretary happened to be my next door neighbor and instead of sending me away she asked me to wait. Before long the president was free. I went in and blurted out my story. To my complete surprise, the president was sympathetic.

More than that, he admitted he didn't like the plant manager and that they were checking him out thoroughly as it appeared he was involved in some serious misconduct. He asked me to sit tight and wait. A month or so later the manager was dismissed from the college and I had my old job back.

How sweet it was that winter to sit back at my desk and go through the lists of supplies, making note of the shortages, the items that needed to be reordered. Sweet and yet, too much had happened. I had had my fill of small town life. That year we sold our property and took the train to Los Angeles. For five years I had lived without palm trees, without orange and lemon blossoms. Exile was over. We had abandoned a windy little town in the heart of the Cascade Mountains.

And the friends we left behind: librarians, professors, neighbors... they went on to fulfill their lives, living behind the curtain of distance, the one thousand colors of silence. Praise be the cottonwood that shades the river. Praise be the ever possible tomorrow, its bearded nature, its clean-shaven laugh.

At the end of that journey lay the Pacific Ocean with its shellfish odor, its vast blue armpit rippling in nervous balance to the days, the moons, the seasons, its great monsters; great curve of earth-breast.

And sunlight! And enough fire below it to broil the imagination of a hundred thousand Eskimos... Imagine the huge ocean beefing up its whales, driving its needle of black ice into the crevice where the slow octopus of lava sleeps. This ocean has islands with volcanoes for shoulders and cool portraits of chaos ready to unveil at the next public swap-meet of the cosmos. The ocean is the mother of mothers, its liquid root a blue speed in the vein. Listen to it when its mouth is silent, for any subsequent speech will destroy your hearing.

> *a heart to heart talk*
> *mother Mrs. Madrepore*
> *and the hot lava*

Imagine it! It belongs to the sub-atomic scale when compared to the whirl of nebulae but it is magnificent and terrifying to those of us of flesh and blood.

As a child I remember profound rivers tunneling through the green growth of a mountain, like quiet snakes in search of their overwhelming mate. Into these, hills urinate with the languor of a professional drunkard. That is the elegance of sleep, of never-ending humidity. But a waterfall can also play with its paw of a cat.

> *leaping at the chance*
> *the waterfall whisks a fly*
> *off the horse's back*

All water ends by having no anatomy, no knees, no height, no lifted voice. And to begin again it grows a heart, a hand, a forehead. In the mountains water is almost always in a hurry; it resembles you, children, you at your games, your mischief, your beauty. Like a mountain, I have embraced you only to have you slide off and join your playmates... your mother.

That journey to Los Angeles took place in 1957. Pigo, you were five and Aglaia, you four. I still remember how you embarrassed me on the train: Directly in back of our seat, a young woman and her daughter were also traveling south. You made friends fast. And in order to amuse the three of you young ones through the endless hours I went through my small repertoire of tricks. You knew them all, but the little girl was enthralled and even her mother took notice.

"Oh, but that's nothing," one of you piped up proudly at the end of a simple card trick, "Daddy can make a penny disappear through his mouth..."

I shrank at what was coming next. "No! No!" I protested, but it was too late, the truth was out of the mouth of babes.

"... and come out of his behind!"

I blushed deeply and couldn't look the young lady in the eye during the rest of the trip although I believe she laughed along with my wife.

DEAR PIGO, FROM THE VERY FIRST WE SAW that you were destined for music. I have never wanted my children to follow paths of my own preference, but in your case it was so obvious that a shoemaker would have had to give in and purchase a quarter-size violin instead of handing you an insole. As a babe in arms you would shed tears whenever I played a particular piece on the phonograph, a Peruvian folk song.

It didn't just happen once; you would cry soundlessly each and every time we played that folk song. Tears would roll down your cheeks. It was no normal crying after an object or for pain or because you had cholic; that music was saying something to you of future anguish; it was a promise of deliverance.

> *a Peruvian song*
> *is all that it takes to set*
> *a child on his path*

Later comes Mozart. Mozart is that moment when you wake to the loss of world and self, the ravishing cleavage with the lost illusion of security on the one side and the immense longing, the immense loneliness, the immense possibility of yet recouping everything through the doors of paradox on the other. You wake at three in the newlywed morning with the loss, so real and tender, of the past... of everything, in other words, that went to shape your assumed solidity in this universe. And you are left with it at a tantalizing distance, with memory the only possible hands that can reach out for comfort. From then on dreams are dreams of castles, of endless staircases spiralling toward an adventure of air and flower, of women lifting their arms in a dance of infinite importance.

You know that there is no hope but to sleep mercilessly with them, carving children from their flesh, devouring their syntax. Mozart is still the tenderness which neither questions nor answers the awakening: men moving toward the steel mill, dawn, flannel, an exclamation, an odor, the skin of air. As in thick mist, there is a separation between peacock neck and peacock tail. Each eye of the fly must repeat nearly the same message but here the tenderness lies not so much in how much one sees as in how much one relinquishes.

> *a day of dark clouds*
> *picketing the horizon*
> *for a silver coin*

Goodbye, sweet moon! I looked at you once, on my way to the Chuey's to read poetry there, and you were already inhabited, the first men were taking a few steps on your carpet of loneliness. Goodbye, moon! Down here a child is listening to Mozart!

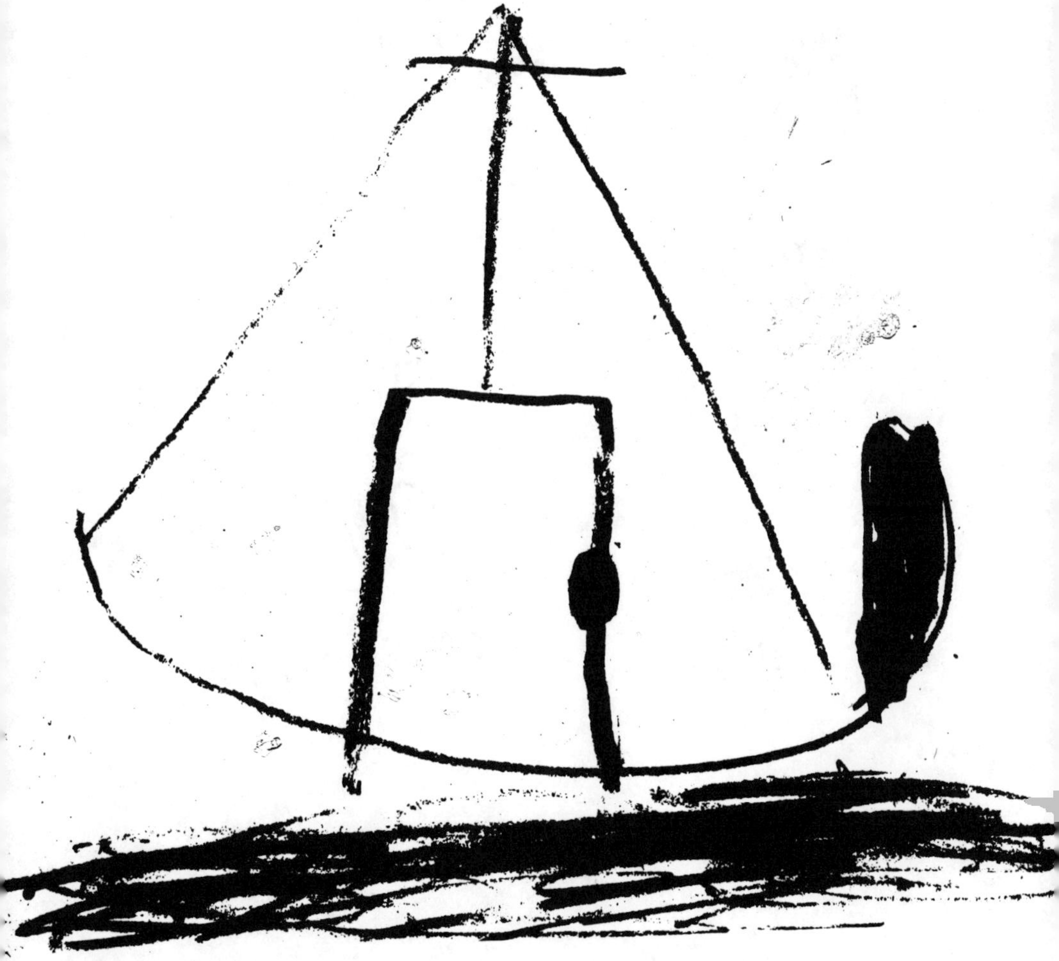

Elena is eight, nine, seven... butterflies come to her party, they become napkins, they sit on her head. And now she's only five and she's frightened; she has heard a bear laugh in her sleep, a mad bear who eats his way through mountains...

"Why?" she cries, "why?"

She has awakened me from a dream in which I glue kisses onto the shoes of my superiors. When I tell her my dream she laughs.

"Let's trade, Daddy! You take my bear..."

I do not tell her that she has no superiors. I kiss her on the forehead and when I get to my bed I punch the bear in the mouth. In the morning, however, I find my shoes chewed up into ribbons.

"Why?" I cry out loud, "why?"

From the Los Angeles train depot, on a fine smoggy day such as only Los Angeles can manufacture, we took a taxi to Norwalk, where my parents and sister were renting a small house. Norwalk is in the middle of forty or fifty square miles of clam chowder industrial horror, emptiness and waste. They import a tawdry semblance of attractiveness in the form of small, square plots of grass, some palms and pink or white oleander. The rest is wire, metal, storage tanks, factories, parking areas, freeways.

In the backyard of that house, such as it was, fierce red ants scurried here and there between the weeds. It was a backyard where you went to hang the laundry, that's all.

None of us cared for that area of Los Angeles. My family had rented that house while waiting for us to arrive from Ellensburg. A month or so later we moved to an old-fashioned, two-story house on Harvard Boulevard near Wilshire, a house soon destined to give way to yet another execrable apartment building.

It was while we were living in that house that I introduced my sister to Lee, the man who would become her second husband. They married and moved to the San Fernando Valley, ultimately drawing the rest of us to that area, on the other side of the dry hills where I had roamed alone during my teens.

The Harvard house possessed some of the things that the American middle class managed to make its own during the first decades of the twentieth century: it was comfortable and roomy, well-built, practical. In the backyard, directly outside the dining room's French windows, there grew a persimmon tree with its fruit weighing it down, the second such tree in my life.

> *the persimmon branch*
> *knows exactly what's inside*
> *the mother's belly*

Many years before, in 1940, when we first went to live in Hollywood, our neighbor in back had a persimmon tree. I had never seen such a delectable creature, so small for the size of the fruit it bore, so solid and green. For some reason persimmons didn't grow in Costa Rica: perhaps they had never been brought in, for the tree obviously loves heat. Maybe it does not like too much water, who knows... The garden where this first persimmon tree of mine grew was, even by middle-class California standards, an incredible oasis of well tended fruit and flower, cared for by a lovely old woman. I'd stand on a box and peer at it over the fence.

> *clouds and persimmons*
> *the sun flaps its wings and crows*
> *over the rooftops*

A few times I did more than look. I could not get over the richness of the fruit; its flesh has the feel of a very tender fish muscle, and it is sweet, overpoweringly so.

> *stolen persimmons*
> *eaten in a quandary*
> *of guilt and sugar*

Our own yard had a fig tree, a pepper tree that I loved to climb, and a grapefruit tree. The grapefruits looked like replicas of winter suns, yellow, cold and aloof; they were quite acid so they stayed on the tree all year long. The figs, on the other hand, were almost always pecked by the blue-jays, and spoiled that way, but I didn't care. Their kind of sweetness didn't attract me. I could never forget Costa Rican figs stewed and dried in sugar, they possessed a perfume somehow lacking in the fresh fruit.

There is something very special about living in a strange new country at the age of thirteen. Everything you see has the impact and immediacy of a blow, a gust of handsome wind. The proximity of pine trees was one such instance. The love with which people took care of their gardens was another. In the tropics nature takes care of itself; nothing has to be tended.

And here I was, having to learn a new tongue in order to get along, to make friends.

> *Simple Simon went a-fishing*
> *for to catch a whale...*

Why *a-fishing?* Why *for to catch?* My grandmother, who had taught me that little rhyme in preparation for California had never explained the weirdness of English to me. It was to be a slow process, learning this capricious language.

The only friend I made those first Hollywood years was a boy named Stormy, freckled and sturdy, who lived half a block away, on a quiet street named Sierra Bonita. The street had a gentle slope to it, the last bit of vertigo descending from the Hollywood Hills and we who built our own wagons and raced down that street knew that vertigo well.

Stormy's father kept parakeets in two large aviaries in his backyard beneath the shade of giant pepper trees. And as if that were not roof enough, grape vines grew all over them with their dusty clusters of small, oversweet fruit.

A good time, a lonely time, when Hollywood Boulevard was a sleepy business street with a few too many movie houses and an odor of recently buried or dying greatness before its crassest hour, World War II and its aftermath.

Now, on Harvard, the same palm trees, the same token sky, less blue, noisier. When I drove past the place we had lived on Hollywood Boulevard, an apartment building sat on the past with the aplomb of a rhinoceros, crushing it permanently. Again, later, driving past Harvard was the same story, as if the jaws of a crane were following close behind our footsteps.

We pretended it was otherwise. The night I came back from reading at Josephine Chuey's house (they had a poetry gathering each last Saturday of the month and, having heard me at my first reading, they had invited me to come)— that night of full moon you, Elena, were conceived. As I say,

> *the persimmon branch*
> *knows exactly what's inside*
> *the mother's belly*

Because Elena was coming, my wife and I decided it was time to rent a separate house. My folks went to live with my sister in the Valley. By now I was working at a huge life insurance company, and a meaner, more tight-fisted outfit would be hard to find. They paid you peanuts and managed to extract the last ounce of work during the eight hours you belonged to them. If you came in late more than a few times in the year you were automatically disqualified from getting a raise. And yet their monetary reserves were monstrously large, as are the reserves of all the large insurance companies in the country: the biggest and most useless reserve of private capital in the world. Fear of insolvency, generated during the bleak days of the early Thirties, brought on such a reaction that every actuary in their employ was put to work to figure ways of loading the premiums of a policy to the hilt. Actuarial science is nothing but the art of usury raised to the square root. They use outdated mortality tables to do the basic computation of a premium and then, by a thousand other tricks, not least of which is the so-called accumulation of cash values, they manage to extract an even bigger bite out of the poor sucker "who knows a good deal when he sees one."

Yes, I was working in an office when you came, Elena. The Irolo house survived between a hedge of hibiscus in front and a tight little garden in back where lots of snails shared the American craze for mobile homes. My late friend Bert Meyers would drop in and watch my urge to paint, or we'd hurl haiku at each other. Once a week I'd go down to the Unitarian Church where Stanley Kurnik had his poetry workshop and we would try to mend a poem's fences, chasing after the non-existing cattle that had escaped.

It was about then that I began to write haiku in earnest. Less than a year before, a student at the Ellensburg college had shown me one of the volumes of Blyth's translations from the Japanese; it was a revelation to see how much could be said in so few syllables. Reading a little Zen and the four Blyth volumes I began experimenting. At first it was easier not to count syllables; I disliked that approach, a dislike which many American poets still feel when they write haiku-like poems. But with a bit of practice the structure of the poem and the poem itself became one. Bert and I, when we couldn't see each other, would write and send each other the haiku we had written that week. He used to write to me on paper singed by his home-made cigarettes and I would write to him on paper stained with intransitive tears. Once, in answer to one of his haiku I wrote:

> *your new haiku*
> *and the moon truly shining*
> *for this old critter*

but that was when I thought that the word *haiku* consisted of three syllables (not that I know any better now!).

> *what the poet does*
> *is tie the syllabic count*
> *of haiku to moon*

*(but what does he do
if instead of orbit they
go into eclipse?)*

My mother and wife pooled their resources to buy the Blyth collection of haiku for my birthday. I poured over those books as well as over his other writings.

Irolo too came to an end. I don't remember exactly why it was that my parents came to live with us before we moved; it may have been that my sister's place was too small. At any rate, when we moved this time my parents went to a house they purchased in the Valley and we went to the Lemp house, the marvelous house I have already described, also in the Valley.

We were moved by an old codger with a large van and he moved us all at once. Father and I rode in style, sitting grandly on a sofa that stuck out of the back. As we were cruising up Highland Avenue just before the Hollywood Bowl, I recall that the two of us were engaged in a conversation about death. Father spoke of his wish to be cremated rather than buried; he hated the notion of worms working their way through his flesh. I promised him that I would take care of that when the time came. I remember clearly how strange it seemed to me at the time that we should be talking so comfortably about death while we rode watching the great shining busyness of the day flowing around us. My father must have surmised that he was entering the final period of his life. But for a few minor outings, he never again left the Valley except to fly with me in a small plane over the beautiful bay in front of Malibu so that I could drop his ashes like dust-thou-art on the forehead of the planet.

*on the shore a man
on the lake an animal
this happens to us*

THERE WAS ONE TREE THAT HAD TO BE CUT, though I don't know why. It was a tree of deliberate height, of suspenseful weight of branch, chiaroscuro at noon; a dense and most maternal tree. But a tree in the passageway of man, which the axe must bite and feed upon.

There is a loud, wet yelp from its initial inks and its large woman runs toward the guns. She is halted by bullets, staggers and falls. The tree sprawls humanly on the ground, its apron of leaves covering its face, arms broken by the impact, exposing orange flesh in band after wedding band, year upon year, one for each child, for each husbanded spring.

All the slight and palely-flowering *roble sabana* trees of the fence (each fence post in Costa Rica automatically turns into a full tree with time) hold barbed-wire hands and wait, sure that today is a St. Bartholomew Massacre of a day, and that nothing will be left standing on the untrimmable hills but those half-baked clouds cavorting like parables of circuses.

Nearby, my rose apple tree will reach over the roof of the house, delicate and dry even in its moments of dalliance with wind and rain. Its origin was a seed in the shape of two testicles, two fists at prayer, that I picked up one foggy day at the park; a seed found among eucalypti, which I brought home to plant in a peach jar, next to my steam engine...

MIGUEL WAS BORN AFTER WE HAD MOVED to the Valley. The count was complete...I remember how the four children would fall asleep, each in his own pocket of dream; how my wife and I would be left bouncing around, the billiards of a family.

There was an extraordinary gap between our Lemp home, its surroundings, and our necessary frugality. The sun, streaming in through the living room windows, found little furniture to sit in and would perforce stretch out on the floor. The kitchen pantry went empty-handed except perhaps twice a month.

> *why is it the squash*
> *has no profile to speak of?*
> *tell me the story*

We entertained ourselves. Over and over we would play Mozart's Turkish March on the phonograph. We danced to it. In the corners of the uncurtained windows, flies would vie for a diet of spiderweb patience and fake Mozartian gaity.

Happiness consisted of taking showers, of watching crows perch on the branches of our pear and almond trees, of bundling Miguel up and taking him outside, of listening to our neighbor call her cat, of bouncing on a bed with ulcer pains. When one of my wife's aunts died, we inherited a few hundred dollars. Immediately, we purchased a piano.

When Pigo was up the piano was a sprinkler; you had to run or you got soaked. And when the sprinkler would go flat we had to call the piano tuner.

He was somewhat stooped and fairly astute, this meek repair man whose frame of reference was a *cordon sanitaire* of sanity, of cliches delivered sotto voce to an enthusiastic crowd of moments while his fingers mumbled their litanies in a Sargasso of wire... Somewhat bent over by what the wind had said to his mother and what Roosevelt had said in the Thirties and by what he thought he had heard with his own ears.

> *thankful to have lived*
> *in a world of ten fingers*
> *the piano tuner*

That first poetry reading that I gave led to many many things. Like the trunk of a tree, dividing, branching out, it gave life to an entire future. It was through Stanley Kurnik that I met Tom McGrath. McGrath was one of the persons in charge of the highly successful series of poetry readings entitled Poetry Los Angeles. At my reading not only did I meet Lee, my future brother-in-law, and the Chueys, but also Stanley and Ruth Kiesel.

Kiesel, a poet with a stethoscope on the chest of children, introduced me to Gene Frumkin. With others, including Keith Gunderson, we eventually formed a tongue-in-cheek group called the Incognoscenti. We got together informally to share our writing, and we gave many memorable readings together.

The Chueys had a large influence on my life. Bob Chuey died in 1978 in a car accident. He was a troubled man but he hid this beautifully behind his kind smile and his nobility. He was a tall, handsome man with a slight limp caused by a bad knee. This made him look less than upright; he seemed to lean forward a bit, and to one side. Bob was an excellent painter; his abstractions were filled with a glowing tenderness, a lyrical use of color. That his work did not sell well is due to the fact that painting in Los Angeles is almost entirely given over to the latest fads. With few exceptions, the galleries on La Cienega carry nothing but work of the worst sort. An artist like Chuey had to go begging. This not so much embittered him —he was ultimately incapable of feeling bitterness— as it saddened and confused him and made him unsure of himself in the last years.

Bob's kindness towards me was exceptional. He always treated me as if I were his equal even though I had just begun to paint and my efforts were a simple and undiluted wallowing. At his wonderful glass house, a house atop Beverly Hills on a high hill overlooking all of Los Angeles and part of the San Fernando Valley, a house designed by Neutra, one always felt that not only Bob and Josephine were welcoming you but that the paintings, the few white walls, the night entering from all sides, the pigments in the studio, the reeds in the sloping yard outside, were delighted with your visit.

For some twenty years I attended their poetry gatherings, seldom missing any one month. How infinitely sad that all of that is gone! Could it be, when I still so distinctly hear the set of bells that Josephine would ring to bring everyone together? Bob would look over at her and stop discussing painting immediately. From all over the house people would drift back to the living room to sit on cushions, anywhere. Those who had brought poetry would hold their breath expectantly, waiting for Josephine to call on them. Good and bad poetry would together create the indelible tapestry of the evening. Afterwards we would tumble down the steep hill in our cars, turning this way and that until we hit the pedestrian groundswell of the city.

Josephine wrote poetry. She courted the world's spiritual leaders. One of the times she and Bob went to a Krishnamurti seminar in Switzerland she gave Gene and me the use of her house so that we could take LSD. Gene took it one sunny day which he spent outside the bright white house examining weeds half way down the hill while I prepared food, played the phonograph and read. The next time I took it and Gene played nursemaid. Gene drew a sketch of me as I lay on a sofa feeling the first discomfiting effects of the drug. It was a wonderful trip. The poet Mel Weisburd joined us about noon; when he and Gene felt hungry they went down to some restaurant. With the house all to myself and the evening coming on I played Mahler's "Der Abschied," the last section from his *Song of the Earth*, and saw how the clouds rounded the earth above the San Gabriel Mountains. They came on from behind, with the greatest delicacy, as if someone were setting a table and was trying to get the tablecloth to fall in place with one masterful stroke. Things went deep blue, so blue that light was left to its own devices.

pierced through with myself
I see the light abandon
its gold on my skin

And you, Bob? Have you found the place where color sings beyond hill and cloud? The place where only light speaks? The glimpse of it I caught at your place and in your work contains your soul.

Because Josephine was so deeply involved with Eastern religion, she was one of the first to know that a dyed-in-the-wool Zen Master had come to roost in town. One day, sure enough, there was this squat, middle-aged Japanese in flying robes inspecting the hill. He had brought a whole retinue of people with him or else Josephine had invited them to meet this curiosity. His chief deputy, a young American with shaved head, seemed the most accessible. I waited till he was standing somewhat alone and went up to him. Together we watched the city below us and made small talk (the only kind of talk that makes for good Zen). Then I made the mistake of asking him what his name was. He turned to me with the look of one who has seen the light and replied, very distantly, "names don't matter." I, of course, was immediately enlightened and bowed low, my heart bursting with the desire to give him a swift kick and send him sprawling down the nameless hill.

while I lie abed
a new haiku summersaults
out of my navel

Oops! Sorry, dear Muse. Next time it will be a little ball of wool that I can weave and pull over your lovely eyes, you hazel-eyed witch, while I make myself presentable with coffee and pluck the harpstrings or romance on the balcony of your inestimable buttocks.

A summer evening is made to sing. A summer morning is made to gargle with salt water and sing. But no one sings (I don't hear them). Only our secret life, buried beneath appearances, sings on and on, a little bent in conversation, a bit damaged from exposure at a glance (we read everything in faces only we prefer to ignore it). It sings its concertos and its symphonies, its cantatas, suites and ultimatums, one thing alone silencing its rill, one thing which in old age begins to taste of vinegar only to leap away sour and magnificent like a final blast of semen.

> *say Mrs. Cartwheel*
> *that axle of yours has dreams*
> *of a little oil*

    Yes, yes, better hurry. Hurry with your coat, hurry with that lipstick, hurry, hurry, hurry. If you are late to his lecture, the professor will frown and lose his train of thought. That's how well he speaks on relaxation, on the art of letting this and that muscle live with its neighbors, never tightening its clothesline into gossip.

> *offhand*
>   *his penis*
> *officiates in the black mass*
> *of her subconscious*

    I'll spend many days by your side, watching the gold of the sun transferred to the tips of the sycamore tree. I'll spend many nights watching dawn come to your hair, silver and evanescent, until I am left with your bones, your teeth and nails. The longest bones I'll hollow into flutes, the short ones I'll give away, and your teeth and nails I shall rattle in your skull.

> *today it's orange*
> *tomorrow lemon yellow*
> *blessed is urine*

    Certain men urinate as if they were holding a loaded pistol. Others look surprised that urine emerges as a result of an operation that is potentially so much more full of adventure. Very few consider that they are holding the cigars so seldom puffed by the lips of women.

> *happy when it's big*
> *unhappy when it's little*
> *my cherished penis*

    Still, we plead for innocent beginnings and, consequently, for purposes that alternate between ecstasy and relief.
    Perhaps if we wore no clothes we wouldn't be bothered by sex the way we seem to be. But we enjoy warmth and elegance and so we pay the price of pretending there is no body beneath the lace, nothing

begging and screaming underneath the cotton.

With our children, my wife and I adopted a wait and see attitude. We thought that when the children began to ask questions would be the time to give them the necessary information. But, of course, save for a few initial probes at too early an age, the questions never came because children pick up on taboos with the antennae of illumined savages.

In a way, the same thing happened with religion. We wanted them to grow up without preconceived notions, as if reality itself were not a notion. But we assumed that as they grew they would be free to study and approach anything they chose in a pure way. The result was that much later, as friendly adults, we have had to sense the sacred together in tentative, fugitive ways. The soul is an instinct but it gets smothered in society, by society. The majority of human beings settle for habit and they love what the churches dish out by way of what should be personal discovery.

With sex, finally and out of desperation, when Aglaia and Pigo were about nine and ten, we took a sex manual out of the library and sat with them at the kitchen table one afternoon, not realizing that this medical, physiological approach of the typical, well-meaning textbook is purely analytical. It dissects sex as if it were a frog in a laboratory. We poured through objective explanations of the procreative act and through various diagrams of the male and female sexual organs done in awful pinks and blues —enough to discourage the strongest nature from ever seeking the solace of the opposite sex.

The children went along with the whole thing in order to humor us. But inwardly they fled at the speed of light. We were talking knowledge, bringing in hard facts, while all along, the children had been learning the most profound set of subterfuges in the world and enjoying their own pace. We merely interrupted this with our galoshes and made it more difficult perhaps, certainly more awkward, for them to develop the hidden subterranean life that allows us to survive in this world. We wanted our children to understand at once, coldly and analytically, functions and rituals that have a million bird claws sunk into everything we do. The inner life of pleasure was laid bare as on an operating table for them, and the mannerisms of love, lust, desire, want and shame were hopelessly disfigured by the simplistic outline of figures in coitus.

The two great halves of the question: the physical (involving getting to know a person, discovering his or her hidden body, caressing it, participating in it) and the emotional-spiritual (the sharing, the ecstasy, the caring and concern) were totally left out of that manual. As if they didn't exist, or could not be taught or discussed.

What should we have done? Perhaps the children should have been, earlier or always, a part of our most intimate life; I don't know. Should children be witness to the ease with which a father slides in and out of a mother's embrace? The manual was insipid, reality too overwhelming.

Our children, whose eyes were themselves forbidding distances, looked at everything we had to show them that day. They frowned, straining to recognize something of themselves in all that Gray's Anatomy, all that scalpel red in front of them.

What their eyes were saying was: "This isn't really how it is, is it? It couldn't be!" And they smiled, sure that the practical joke we were playing on them would come to an end. But no, the Santa Claus of the body was murdered. The gifts that come down the Christmas chimney are an allegory of the sex function we don't know how to pass from one generation to the next. The result, I suspect, is that we then overestimate male and female relationships, creating a gigantic romantic bubble out of it. When that bubble bursts we have divorce. Sooner murder an infant in its cradle than nurse unacted desires, Blake said.

> *the baker himself*
> *is the best man to tell you*
> *the bread is burning*

MY CHILDREN, THOSE REAL AND THOSE OF CLAY, come to ask me about Schubert. They have heard *Death and the Maiden*, they have heard Opus 53. And they want to know —is it true that he lived, is it true that he died at thirty-three, is it true that as a boy he had to practice for hours in a freezing room, is it true that because he lived the blue foot of the sky got stuck in a horizon of honey...

"Children, children..." I say to them. "I can't answer so many questions all at once; I can't answer a single one of your questions...Can't you see that I have to get dinner?"

I pull a drawer open and there are the onions. They have not been exactly hibernating.

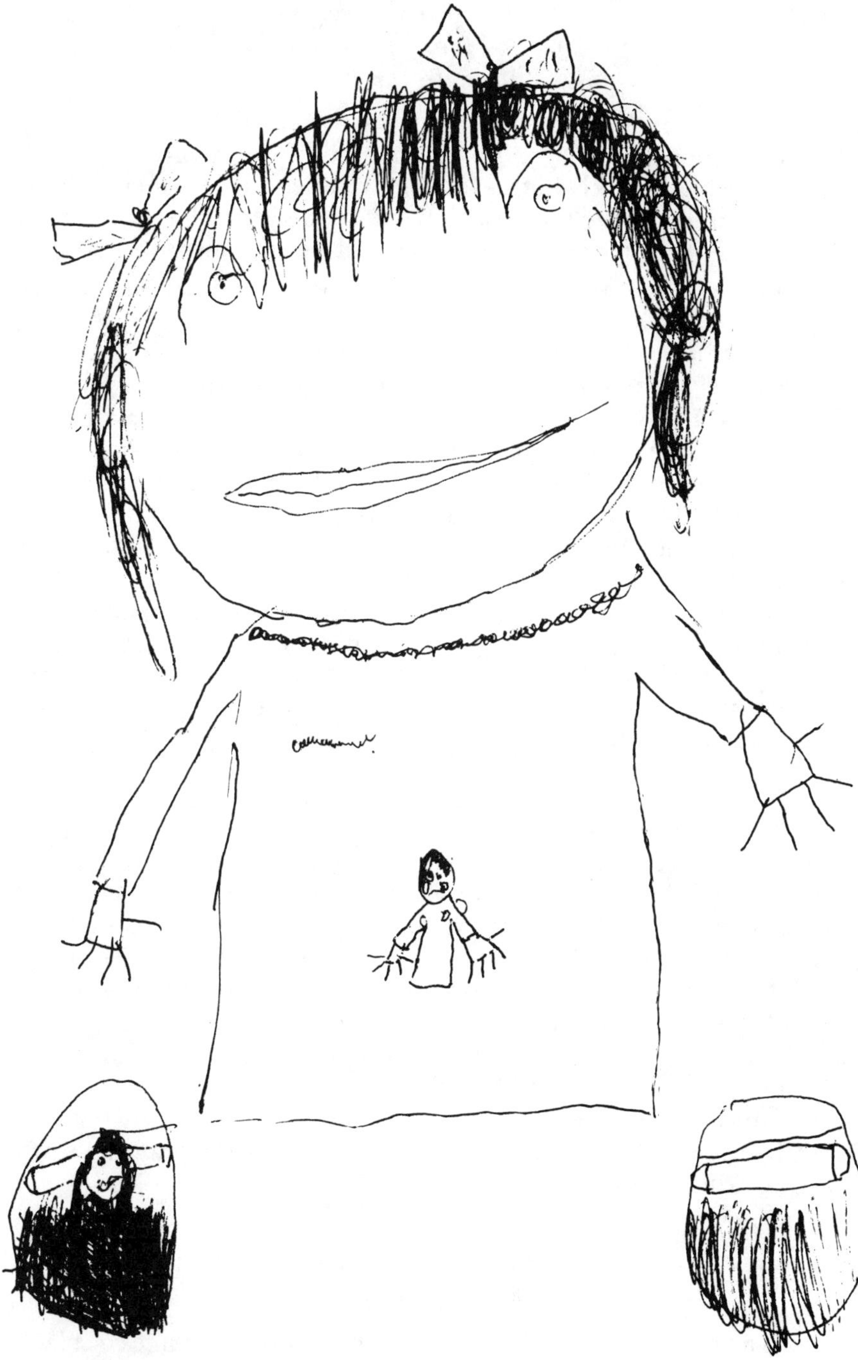

> *some going ahead*
> *with plans for a family*
> *onions in the bin*

    I start the hominy stew, then turn and make rice the way my father taught me: a bit of oil in the pan, some onion, green pepper. The rice is fried briskly in this for a few moments then water is added to half an inch above the top. You salt to taste then let it boil until the water goes down level to the rice and a dozen volcanoes sputter less and less. It's time to cover it and let it simmer for twenty minutes.

    The children have invited Schubert for dinner. If I had known this I'd have thrown in a few prunes and sliced carrots into the rice. But it's too late. I wonder if Schubert likes hominy. Aglaia reminds me that we have a bottle of wine saved for a special occasion. Sure now of the success of our dinner, I direct the happy traffic: "Elena, go get some flowers from the garden! Miguel, you set the table! Pigo, please find me the corkscrew! Aglaia, go put on your lavender dress...!"

    Schubert arrives; he's in a hurry. For a moment I think he's got to use the bathroom, he's jumping around so, but it isn't that. In broken English he explains that he's got to jot down an idea that came to him on the way over. Pigo gives him music paper and pencil and the piano starts and stops, starts and stops, just like our station wagon.

    While that's happening we go back to the kitchen to put the finishing touches on our dinner. Aglaia's eyes are shining. "That is really Schubert in there!" she half asks, half asserts, pointing to the living room. I nod. At that moment the music begins in earnest, never to stop. "You will grieve and you will laugh," it says; "you who must laugh and lose a strand of fear in the wind in order to love laughter. You will grieve with the only sound that angels heed, the sound that comes from the all-stops-open flute of the throat."

    "There are only two kinds of human beings," I explain to the children, "those who sing and those who do not..."

    "Sing...?" they ask.

    "Doing something well is singing, singing the way the earth does, or the odor of coffee"

> *after the earthquake*
> *the smell of coffee takes on*
> *the shape of the roof*

    It's a very simple thing; it's what the floor of any stage could tell you:

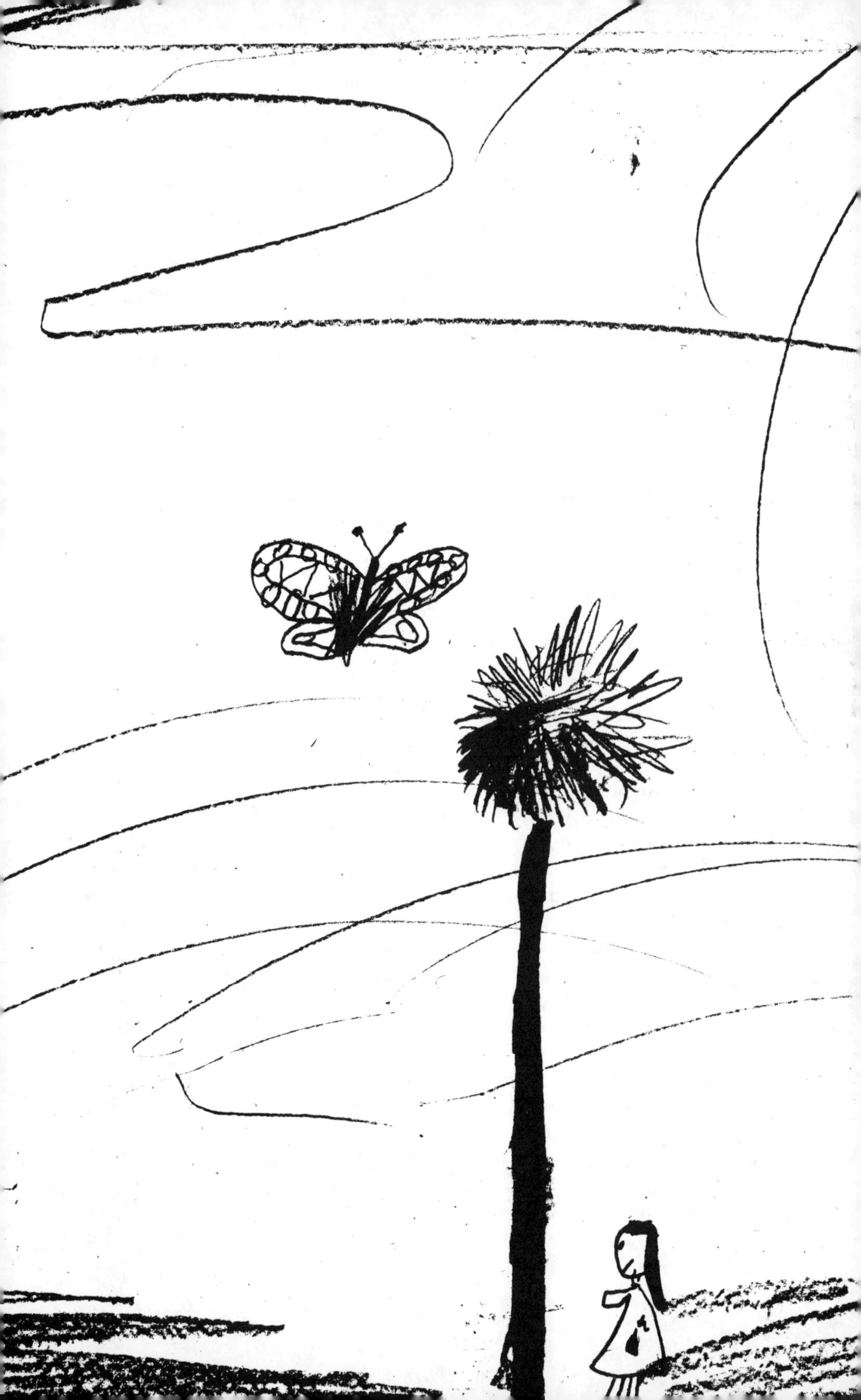

> *the dancing girl knows
> that mountains are interested
> in taking lessons*

We have to keep Schubert from overeating. The children take him outside to play hide and seek while I do the dishes. When they come in, tired and happy, there is not one Franz Schubert but four: each of these four Schuberts is an exact replica of one of my children!

They go through their baths and I put them to bed. As they fall asleep I see each of them smile into dream: Pigo-Schubert smiles, Aglaia-Schubert smiles, Elena-Schubert smiles, Miguel-Schubert smiles. I collect these smiles and go to my desk, remembering that I have to work on a poem.

> *the singer begins
> when there's no world and no throat
> to do the singing*

CHILDREN, DO YOU REMEMBER THAT ELEPHANT at the zoo who decided to pee in public? Well, some things are best done extemporaneously like that. The most wonderful thing that happened to me on my way to be a father was the fact that it was so unplanned. Not one of you four children was asked for or denied. I don't recall that your mother and I ever sat down and discussed whether we should have children or not. This may seem hard to believe but we were young and lived in an age in which planned parenthood was a very new concept. Besides that, we had formed no concepts about how life should be lived. If you, Elena and Miguel, were more difficult to accept when first conceived and discovered hiding in the briar patch of the imminent future, and for purely economic reasons, we quickly came round to the wonder of seeing the new life that was so much ours and so much itself. Elenita, you were a very sweet mouse from the first even if you did fuss at night the way Pigo and Aglaia had. When you came, Miguel, the fact that we now had two boys and two girls made us enormously happy.

I had wanted to be present at your birth because I knew you would be my last child (in the same way —exactly— that I had not known I would have four children). Unfortunately, the head night nurse at the hospital was most adamant, a regular German elephant, unjust and bluish and wishing to be incorporated into my general papers as a sort of contiguous neighbor who will lend you salt and cooking utensils now and then and who will come over for tea and be too polite to mention her superior knowledge of brands but who can't help herself, goes home and gives vent to her contempt by beating her servants.

She was unjust and bluish. When I asked to see the birth she said it was not a thing for a man to see. Definitely not an elephant who believed in public peeing. I had no recourse but to go home and await developments. The elephant had assured me that the child would not be forthcoming until early the next morning. But lo and behold, along about three in the morning the telephone rang. It was the hospital telling me I was a father. My joy extinguished my anger at the pachyderm.

> *this elephant pees*
> *with no concern for the fact*
> *that God is looking*

That same hospital had been upset a few years before when Elena was born and we had no name to give her; we just hadn't made up our minds about it. It got to be time to take the child home and still no name. They let her go reluctantly, as if they could have kept her! The original records show only her little footprint. A few days later we settled for Elena, which was my paternal grandmother's name, and sent the hospital word.

> *do photographs lie?*
> *a year and a half later*
> *I smell the perfume*
> *you have become a flower*
> *smelling another flower*

You don't recall that, Elena, but you posed for me ever so nicely, on the side garden of the Lemp house. I asked you to smell a flower and you took a deep breath, one you are still holding.

Miguel was the best behaved at night. He made up for it during the day! When my half-brother Alfredo first visited us he couldn't get over Miguel's pranks. He was worse than a puppydog at the chewing stage, with a roguish smile you couldn't resist.

> *uncle and nephew*
> *the only language they know*
> *is Charlie Chaplin's*

My brother was to come several more times in the course of the years. Always to visit our ever older father, stay one or two weeks and purchase American clothes. On that first visit Pigo was already so impressive on the violin that Alfredo impulsively gave him a tiny pre-Columbian rabbit made of onyx... the same rabbit that Miguel would go after in the rocky gullies just outside Albuquerque.

Since Father and Mother eventually settled in a cabin behind my sister's now ample house, Alfredo subsequently came and stayed with Ana on his periodic visits. We'd have grand parties there, around the pool where Miguel almost drowned one night before I taught him how to swim.

My sister, I want to say this here, no matter what her poverty, always manages to be munificent. If she has to steal she will but no one is ever turned away from her table, her open arms. She has always worked hard; she has dreamed with her head to one side, listening to her six children. Her dreams are combinations of glory and housework, mountains of laundry and continents of sound. She knows how deep a well should be if it is to produce cool water, and at what phase of the night a star will shine reflected on that coolness.

the empty courtyard
clouds and the song of a bird
shut away somewhere
if my sister were a nun
I would call sister sister

The last time Alfredo came to visit Father was the most poignant. Each time, of course, it was hard on both of them because each thought privately it would be the last time they'd see each other. Alfredo was always deeply affected and this time he confessed to me that he would not return again. The night before he left, we turned chance into a sort of intense family efflorescence.

We were all present at the dinner my sister had prepared. Lee had read, in some film magazine or other, that Melico Salazar, my father's long-dead cousin and one-time world famous tenor, had made a short film just at the onset of sound. Portrayed on the screen was the crucial scene from Verdi's Othello when Othello kills Desdemona. Checking with a film warehouse, Lee discovered that they had a print of this historic film. After much maneuvering, he managed to rent it the night of our dinner, the day before Alfredo was to fly back to Mexico. At twenty minutes to five, just as we were getting ready to come over for the party, Lee asked me if I could locate a film projector. His wasn't working. There was a rental company near us and I rushed there minutes before closing time. I obtained the last machine they had and arrived at my sister's with it. After dinner we set up chairs in rows as in a theatre, sat down and, with the room emotionally charged and dark, started the machine.

There, months before his own death, my father was able to see his dead cousin once again and to hear him at the height of his powers. We were in awe of his voice and of this strange way of vaulting over time and space. My brother had his memories of the great singer, as did my mother and even I. I recall him, an older and by then defeated man —defeated by high living— sitting on the front steps of his sisters' house in our old San Jose neighborhood. It was on a Sunday and Father and I were out walking when there he was, a paunchy, much-lived man with an immense bulge between his legs made prominent by the tightness of his pants. Father always remembered that as youths, in a silly fight over some inconsequential issue, Melico had almost choked him to death with his bare hands. And yet, at one time, his voice rang all over the operatic earth with the tenderness of an emerald.

> *back in his home town*
> *he suns himself in the shade*
> *of his sisters' house*

That dinner, when we witnessed Salazar on film, happened seven years after I had left wife and children and was living with my present wife. Everyone was reconciled, almost happy. It was my father's death that scattered the family to the four winds: my sister and mother first to Indiana and then to New York while her two older children stayed behind in Los Angeles; my wife and I to Minnesota; Aglaia, Elena and Miguel in Los Angeles with their mother; Pigo roving the country. Currently, Pigo has been with me, transcribing a violin concerto I have written. In turn, my father, in my dreams, has told me he will help me if I am sincere. Indeed, since 1975, my life has opened up incredibly.

> *after Father died*
> *this river without a shore*
> *turns into a bridge*

Steel bridges are so much less real! There is, first of all, a bridge to be crossed on a nothing day when, once more, I must attempt to sell insurance. At home we barely make ends meet. In my heart I am desperate...

That bridge connects Downtown and East Los Angeles; does it while the city behaves as if it didn't matter, the smog reflected on the oily pools of the water. The sky is laden with grey and in the span of a second I dream of a locomotive traveling across the vast expanse of a prairie under a foot of snow, it alone knowing where the rails lie.

> *riding home from work*
> *falling asleep in the midst*
> *of one more haiku*

Many times, riding the bus from Downtown to North Hollywood, I would attempt to read or write but would almost invariably fall asleep. I was tired to death in those days; I was always miserable but alive, searching for insight, for patience.

> *looking for a key*
> *finding a missing haiku*
> *in the old jacket*

IF YOU HAVE EVER MOVED AROUND THE WORLD, sometimes you will find —to your great surprise— that the sun sets on what you feel is the wrong side, that it rises where it shouldn't.

Living in Los Angeles, in the Lemp house with a glass wall facing a relocated east, many mornings I would be bathed by the first orange rays of the sun while ironing a shirt for the day. Our parakeet, that fist of blue, would begin to chirp and celebrate its little bag of longevity, hacking at grains of feed with its hooked bill.

> *ironing a shirt*
> *my parakeet and daybreak*
> *the two companions*

One day, bluer than all the others, I found that parakeet dead against the world. I buried it under the peach tree, thinking that the tree would have trouble flowering pink the next spring.

> *check it out*
> *children*
> *is there any trace of blue*
> *in that singing peach?*

IN THE HEART OF LOS ANGELES THEY HAVE TORN down some of the old buildings and left others standing at attention. Look how that one in particular, with its neighbors' pants down, shows a splendid and almost limitless expanse of brick where time has worked its abstractions. Look at those dishevelled stains, that great abandonment and skill! What painter could possibly do as well? Nevertheless, no one looks up; or if they look, they don't see, don't enjoy. To them it's a dirty old brick wall. They walk by with their shopping bags full of worry, themselves magnificent stains upon the limitless meaning of the spirit, and don't look.

> *early evening*
> *a lone cricket masturbates*
> *without compunction*

AT THE MILL THEY ARE STIRRING THEIR VATS of honey. When it is all done, the brown sugar will be stacked in truncated cones some five inches in diameter. As a child I understood the whole process, from the sticky heat of the sugarcane fields to those cones we worried with knives to get at our sugar. In the San Antonio mill there was a worker who could dip his hand into the boiling, wheat-colored inferno, that blazing cauldron, and bring up a sizzling beehive of the stuff for us to chew. Quick as lightning he'd dip his hand into a pail of water...

Contrast that to the goosepimples on a boy emerging from the shower. The water is always icy; when I was young we never knew what it was to have hot water to bathe in.

Listen children, you are the hair that grows upon your arms and legs, ten times over. You are the purpose of your twenty nails, the shadow cast upon the ground and which the ants traverse, wondering at the eclipse.

> *look how the ants come*
> *single file and yet living*
> *all in the present*

I find it strange, bewildering even, that the present should include the ant filing before me, the ant preparing to do so, and the one just emerging from its hole in the ground. If you're not with it, cross yourself, seek sanctuary, another form of payment.

> *going for a walk*
> *with a perfectly silent*
> *coin in my pocket*

Did I give you enough spare change, children? Did I pamper you a bit, buy you enough digestive disasters to qualify as a good father? As a child I seldom had enough; I envied neighborhood kids their toys, their ability to summon street vendors at will.

But having nothing is our own doing. One day, tired of our dog, after he had eaten your entire birthday cake, Aglaia, when your mother had looked the other way, I took him to a well-to-do neighborhood, and let him out. I didn't want any more to do with him, I felt he had gone back on his deal with us whereby we fed and housed him and he protected us. Lord, as if he wasn't entitled to some weakness!

At times I have suspected that there is actually little love in my heart, little warmth when it comes right down to it. You children must have missed the dog, though you never said a word that I can recall. Were you scared of me?

I used to punish you once in a while, when we felt that you really deserved it. Always afterwards such violence left me with a bad taste in my mouth. How much damage did I cause? And can one go back afterwards and repair it? I hope there was enough richness in each of your childhoods to make up for the deficiencies. I was not there in school with you, I never saw enough of your days. Did you have a school life as wonderful as mine was? At night I was grouchy, tired, seeking the solace of my writing desk, imagining that I could write a poem that would come to make it all right.

After I left, how difficult it was to come and pick you up to go somewhere! Pigo, you seldom came, you were busy with your music and school sports. What to do with three children each five years apart in age? We'd go to the beach, to movies, to amusement parks; once we went to Bert Meyers' house in Claremont...

One evening, Elena, just as I left you at your front door, you and Miguel begged me to come back. As if one can ever go back to what once was! But I will always feel that I never gave you what you most desired, my heart as shield for life's battles. And yet, of course I gave it, that thin, useless shield!

I began writing this book (long ago) thinking that I could speak and write about us, talk about us as if I knew definite things about ourselves. But especially with your own children you make the mistake of thinking you know who they are. We humans only manage to bring mysterious beings into this world, beings whom one can know only a little better than one knows a passerby on the street. I have tried to resurrect the years shared with you only to find that they were ghostly to begin with. And it's no use regretting this; on the contrary, it is a point of departure, an awareness that generates its own magic freedoms.

Knowing that I desperately want to recapture the warmth of gone days with you and knowing that it can't be done, I still lay claim to my human, my handicapped, my imperative love for you. And through that imperfect love for you I am dimly aware that nothing at all has been lost. On the contrary, that somehow because of my giant failure, love and event were somehow perfect and real.

> *look*
> *we have grown tall*
> *let it be our breaths that free*
> *the dandelion*

```
PS           Cardona-Hine, Alvaro.
3505
A6.55        When I was a father.
W4
1982
```

**NORMANDALE
COMMUNITY COLLEGE**
9700 France Avenue South
Bloomington, Minnesota 55431